THE JOURNAL OF

SILAS POPE

A 19th Century Thaumagere

Translated and compiled by
Ken Reynolds

British Occult Secret Service

Archive reference: #05072013-DJKR

First Printing, 2020
e-Book Release, 2020

ISBN 979-8-65770-618-5

www.kenreynolds.co.uk

Illustrations by
Adam Jakes

From the world of

⚕⚕⚕⚕⚕⚕⚕

Every operative that achieves a certain standing within a secretive and unusual organisation like the British Occult Secret Service, will be offered a device for *motus effusio.* The other apprentices used to call them 'Sentiment Stones'.

I am no different.

Some choose not to use them, believing themselves to be made of stern stuff; unflappable and stalwart. Most soon discover there are things in, and beyond, this world that would make a marble statue soil itself. Unfortunately those same agents don't tend to last long enough to see the error of their ways.

The mind is a Thaumagere's greatest strength, and their most vulnerable weak-spot. The mind must be kept sharp and clear. The job in hand is always paramount, the past irrelevant. The present moment and how it affects the future is all there can possibly be.

Having said this, the past cannot be ignored for its instructive qualities. We learn from our experiences and our mistakes, but such things can be shrouded with negative emotion. These memories can be the rocks that weigh us down, causing us to drown.

My mentor developed the Sentiment Stone as a way to condition his recruits. I daresay he had been dabbling with it for many years himself. It would certainly explain his swift, singular advancement.

I recall the morning that he visited me. I was barely a man myself. I had seen things early in my life that cannot be unseen. It was decided I had promise, that resources would be diverted to shape me into something more. But to justify the expense I had to fully commit, to supplicate myself to the process.

My mentor was not unkind. As he slid the smooth oval crystal towards me, he explained the risks and promised two things; I would never have nightmares again, and I would do terrible, but great, things.

He spoke truthfully, but I don't believe for a second even he could have guessed what lay before me in a varied career of unspeakable horrors.

It would seem very odd to an outside observer for a spy to take the time documenting his activities in detail - an obvious security risk. This was a primary concern when the process was explained to me. Spy-craft, in many ways, has similarities to the nature of magic; subtleties that only the practitioner can be aware of, and which the observer will never realise or understand. It all comes down to superior knowledge. Science can seem like magic to the uninformed. Magic quite obviously seems like magic to most, but it is only because of its broadly unknown mechanics. To be a successful spy is to be able to keep secrets, to retain and withhold knowledge for your own benefit and to fiercely guard that knowledge because your life, and the life of many others, will depend upon it.

This manuscript is written on paper pulped with protective elixirs; the ink I use can only be read by my eyes. The folio I keep the manuscript in has been stamped with all manner of glyphs to make it impossible for any other hand to touch it. All of this is nothing when compared to the protections I have set around my personal safe. So it is with a clear conscience that I write these thoughts, as they are for an audience of one, never to be re-read and only existing for the practical mechanics of self-preservation. In fact, I doubt that much sense would be made if these pages were readable by another. I have never used dates for reference, as placing these events in history means very little to me. I'm sure some situations would be easily recognisable, though it would inevitably lead to further confusion, as the span of my life would soon seem rather improbable. In addition to this, each time I open the folio to add a new entry it seems the pages have somehow shifted order. They are certainly not in any sensible chronology.

As I render these words to the page, I hold in my writing hand the Sentiment Stone. The action of writing is a singular one. It is a record of memories and experiences unique to the writer. Thoughts and feeling flow from the mind, through the hand and scrivening utensil, to be seeded onto a page. There is something elemental in this action; it is not simply the summation of ink soaking into fibre.

The Sentiment Stone works as a filter; it collects all of the emotion connected to the content of the writing. As I am recording my own experiences and memories, I am effectively removing my feelings from them. I get to keep my recollections of past events without being weighed down by them. I can subjectively assess my successes and failures coldly and precisely without my judgement being clouded.

This is the price that must be borne to be successful in my vocation.

I have concerns about how much of my humanity is skimmed by the process, but sacrifices must be made so that the majority of people need never take similar actions.

It takes monsters to battle monsters and I'm glad to be one such monstrosity that is on the side of good.

I cannot conceive of any possible situation in which another soul might read these words. If it has come to pass, I can but imagine the dire circumstances in which the reader might find themselves. I'm certain I would be judged sternly for my actions in the tales I recount, though it is nothing compared to the judgements I pronounce upon myself.

Upon the completion of my life I know precisely where I'm headed; I also know I will have saved countless others from the same fate.

- - - - - - -

Mixed in with these papers you may find some drawings. Unfortunately they are not from my own hand, they are sent to me from a gentleman named Jakes.

I helped him some time ago. He came to my attention when he helped the local constabulary solve a series of child abductions.

Jakes draws things he sees in his dreams. Sometimes they are disturbing in nature, but they are always an accurate reflection of life. The things he draws occur, have occurred, or will occur at some time in the future. He tells me that visions of the future are rare though.

After I met him, and decided to leave him be as he posed no threat to anybody, he took to sending me pictures that involved myself.

It seems that whatever power is behind his abilities took a liking to me and my activities. Sometimes I will get a picture that could be a scene from my past, distant or recent, occasionally I get one that feels like a warning as I do not recognise its contents.

I try to include images that relate to the events I record, but sometimes I hide them away as they feel too sensitive.

I am no art critic, but there is a small part of me that feels it is a shame Jakes' work will not reach a wider audience, even if their creation is uncanny.

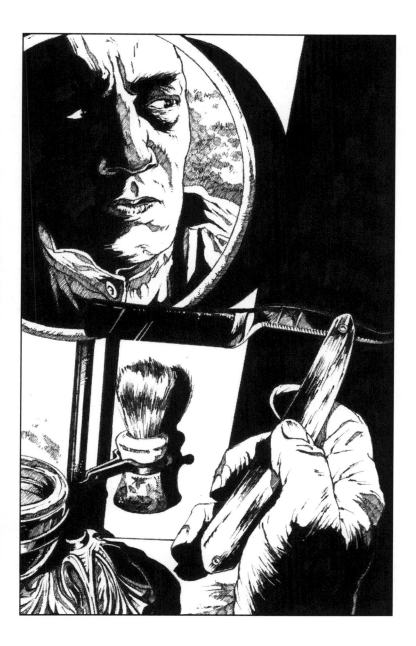

₺ ₺₺₺₺₺ ₺₺ ₺₺₺₺ ₺₺₺

I was settled at my desk, clutching my Sentiment Stone, ready to exorcise my emotions attached to the latest run-in with Victor Souriant (Codename: 'L'Effroi'). I never seem to gain the upper hand over that man. It vexes me.

It would have been to my advantage if I could have taken some time to get it all out of my system. As it was, I was still very emotional and not as well prepared for the unexpected test that presented itself.

There was a polite knock at the door; a knock instantly recognisable as that of Jarvis. I've often marvelled that he can communicate so much through rapping his knuckles upon solid wood. He has an urgent knock, a discreet knock, even a warning knock. This one was quite generic and simply insisted permission to enter.

I grunted my assent. He knew my noises as well as I knew his.

Jarvis entered the room smoothly, I barely noticed that the door had opened and closed, he simply appeared this side of it. It was actually more astonishing because I knew for certain he didn't use magic to do it.

"Sorry to disturb you, sir. You have a visitor - a young Lady in need of your assistance. I don't believe she has an appointment, but she was referred here by Detective Hailwood."

Percy Jarvis has been with me for many years. He has seen more horrors by my side than most others of my acquaintance. That alone should vouch for his tenacity and varied skills, for he has survived. He didn't used to be older than me, but he will now forever look it, as the years have eroded him and slid by me. His posture is still ramrod-straight, and the bearing of his head has never been anything less than proud. His has been a life of service and thus quiet, mostly unrewarded heroism.

The mention of the detective caught my attention. It would have burned him to recommend my expertise. I had helped him in the past, but he never liked to admit his limitations. I began to tidy away my things into the desk draw. Slid my papers into a folio stamped with protective runes, tied the string into a knot only I could loosen, and sealed it with wax, that if broken by any other hand than mine would make the writing on the parchment unreadable. I also returned my Sentiment Stone to its case and snapped the lid closed. I locked the desk draw, placed the key in my waistcoat pocket and whispered an enchantment to strengthen the mechanism.

"The lady's name, Jarvis?"

"Lady Mabel Proctor, sir."

"Of 'The Proctors'?" I asked.

"I believe so, sir. From Lincolnshire, I'm told. In town for a family bereavement. I believe it is pertinent to her enquiry."

"Very good, please show her in. Bring us some refreshments, if you would."

"Of course, sir."

Again, the door barely moved as Jarvis exited.

I stood to receive the lady, casting a quick eye around the room for anything that I might have inadvertently left lying around. An idle action, as I knew full well there was nothing, but years of habit are impossible to break. Past lessons were taught harshly, and my habits formed as a preventative.

I was under no illusions when the door opened again. I worried for the hinges.

Lady Proctor stormed into my office; to say she was perturbed would be an understatement. I know it is polite to say women 'glow', but she was virtually frothing like a horse. Wearing a black mourning dress and veil she strode across the room, plunged a hand into her bag, and slammed a small book onto my desk. Then she turned away from me and retreated across the room; as far away as it was possible to get.

"My sincere apologies, Mr Pope. I realise this is a rather strange introduction, but might I request that if you have a secure drawer or cupboard you might lock that foul volume out of my sight?"

Jarvis came into the room, and with the merest hint of a sly smile said: "May I present Lady Proctor to see you, sir. I'll fetch some refreshments."

Once we were alone I decided to play along and stowed the book in the bureau to the side of my desk. I happened to be next to the drinks cabinet. "May I offer you a sherry, my lady?"

As soon as the book was out of sight and the lock on the bureau had clicked, a quite astonishing transformation occurred. The young lady lifted her veil, and was instantly composed. "Brandy if you have it, please?" At least, outwardly.

I poured the drink and proffered a seat. I have two very comfortable chairs in the centre of my office for informal meetings. People do tend to be at ease without a desk in the way. I offered her tobacco; she declined and proceeded to take some snuff, which was a mild surprise.

I was quite comfortable sitting in silence, letting Miss Proctor gather herself. Between the drink and the powder she was gathering her wits. By the time she seemed ready to speak, Jarvis entered once again with a tea tray.

It was a good ten minutes between the lady's entrance and her beginning to state her business. I must admit I was very interested to hear what she had to say.

"My apologies again, Mr Pope. I meant no offence, and I hope in the telling of my story you will understand my distress. The tale cannot begin with it, but I hope you will bear in mind that what you have seen of me thus far is starkly out of character and speaks to the grave danger I have brought to your door."

"Not at all, Lady Proctor. No need to apologise. Please, tell me what troubles you."

"As you can tell, my family has recently been visited by death. I travelled down to the capital to attend to my grandmother. In truth, it was with a little relief that I received the news. She had become somewhat of a recluse after my grandfather died two winters ago. She would take to her library and stay there for days, getting the staff to bring her meals, even making up her bed there. She was a voracious reader and had pressed my grandfather into assembling one of the most impressive private libraries in the country.

"She was prone to malady, always suffering with pain in her feet and hands. Some days she could barely turn the pages of the books herself, and would have someone stand by to do it for her.

"Despite it all she was always kind and thoughtful. We corresponded regularly, and she always took an interest in my life in Lincolnshire. I believe she had been quite instrumental in making my match, and wanted to keep a close eye on its providence. We always like to see the results of our own handiwork flourish, don't we?"

"Indeed," I replied. "I trust your own immediate family are all well?"

She flushed a little. "Thankfully, they are and they have been fortunate not to be part of these current troubles. I will find it… difficult to explain to my husband. He is not a fanciful man."

"Fanciful? You seem to doubt your own judgement."

Lady Proctor's face became stern. "I do not doubt my own experiences, simply my husband's capacity to accept them. He is a kind man, but he chooses a very narrow and simple view of the world."

She stopped to sip her tea, a tiny crease of disapproval passed like a fleeting shadow across her brow, but she was too polite to pass comment.

"Would you like another brandy?" I offered.

"That would be most welcome, thank you." She adjusted her position on the seat and smoothed her dress. I thought I could sense a bit of trepidation.

"Feel free to continue. Detective Hailwood must have informed you that I have some expertise in strange matters. There is no need to fear disbelief or ridicule from these quarters. We usually deal with three or four unbelievable experiences before lunch." I handed the young lady her drink, which she sipped gratefully.

"So I received the letter from my mother to inform me that Grand-mama had passed away. I recall the phraseology she used, only because of how events unfolded. She wrote: 'Grandmother passed away peacefully in her sleep. She was in the library among her beloved books. In fact, she was still clutching the last thing she read.' I was comforted by the picture Mother painted. It seemed an ideal ending for her.

"Of course, I travelled down at once. I insisted that I come alone. My husband had the estate to attend to, and I didn't think it appropriate for the children to come along. They are a bit too young, and I wanted their final memories of their great-grandmother to be happy ones.

The funeral went as well as these things ever can. Socialising with the near entirety of any extended family will only be pleasant for a finite amount of time. We may all have blood in common, but we diverged a long time ago. Small gripes and petty agendas emerge. Old alliances and scores reassert themselves. Mix that in with the possibility of an inheritance, and the atmosphere becomes charged in a noxious manner.

"Grandchildren, nephews and nieces were handed trinkets, things to remember Grand-mama by. I was lucky enough to get the letters I had sent her back, so I had a complete record of our correspondence. Something I will treasure forever.

"The main stipulation in her will was really quite moving. She asked that each of us enter her library and choose a volume for ourselves to keep, and perhaps start our own literary collection.

"I chose a book of fairy tales that I can share with my children, so their great-grandmother can once again give them a bedtime story."

"How lovely," I commented. I could feel it building. There was tension in the lady's shoulders.

"Quite." Lady Proctor took a longer sip of the brandy. "I stayed here for a week to comfort my mother, make sure she had any help that might be needed to take care of Grand-mama's affairs. Mother is the matriarch now. It is a heavy mantle to bear at her age, and without Father's support. He was taken far too early, when I was a girl.

"We were arranging new sets of mourning clothes just before I was planning to return home. I like to get my clothes from London when I have the chance, and I would be committing to wearing black for at least six months. It was then that further terrible news reached us.

"Cousin Mortimer had been found dead. We were absolutely stunned. He was a young, vigorous man, only nineteen. He hadn't settled down yet. I suppose he was seen as a bit of a wild child, but the boys in our family have always got a lot of latitude on that score. A bit of a right of passage, or so I'm told.

"The shock did not stop there, however. It was reported that he had been found in the precise way Grand-mama had been discovered; as though he had passed away in his sleep, clutching the very same book.

"The book I have asked you to lock away." Her lip began to tremble as she held back tears. I sensed there was more than bereavement behind it.

Lady Proctor mastered her emotions. "Of course, we had to involve the authorities. It cast questions over Grandmother's death, which threw the validity of the will into uncertainty. It's been an ugly time for the family.

"Doctors couldn't properly determine a cause of death. It was deemed natural causes - his body simply stopped."

She drained the remainder of her brandy. "I took possession of the book, on behalf of my mother. The police weren't interested, but I had an unwholesome feeling about the one object that linked the deaths. I left the volume on my dressing table. Each time I glanced at it my stomach turned; I assumed it was simply a mental link to the loss of my family members.

"I prolonged my stay here. My mother was distraught and the strain of managing the family was wrought upon her face each morning. With each passing day my mind would turn more and more to the book on my dresser. At first I found it curious. Then enticing…"

"Then it began to scare you?" I asked.

"Yes, Mr Pope. Yes it did. I found that the book was constantly on my mind. When I wasn't near it I thought about it; when close to it I had a compulsion to pick it up, simply hold it. The longer I held it, the more I felt compelled to open it and read.

"I caught myself opening the cover and threw it across the room. Then I contacted Detective Hailwood. He heard me out and suggested that I seek out your advice. Which brings us up to date.

"The strain of bringing the book to you very nearly overwhelmed me. I do not know what power that book could possibly hold, but I have no doubt that it is malign and had a part to play in taking two members of my family from me."

I'll admit to being surprised. It was something I hadn't heard of before, which is rarer than I might like. When I stumble upon something new it is usually horribly dangerous.

"Would you like me to investigate the book or simply destroy it?" I asked. "You seem quite sure that it is the cause of your misfortunes."

The lady was slightly taken aback. "I suppose I would like confirmation that my suspicions are correct. Otherwise in the time to come I might find myself doubting my own thoughts. But yes, once you've found all you can from the object itself I

believe it would ease my mind to know that it were destroyed...
even if you found that it was innocent and inert."

I promised to do my very best, and that I'd call on her to
report my findings as soon as could be arranged. Her spirit
was considerably lighter when she left my office, as though a
burden had been lifted, quite possibly passed along.

Once I was alone I sat back down to my writing. I got a
good way into it, and found myself hankering for a drink. I
sidled over to the bureau to pour myself a tot and returned
to my desk. I'm not one for excess, but during the afternoon
I made the same trip across the room for a drink on three or
four occasions.

Jarvis called twice; once to leave me some lunch, again to
collect the untouched tray, which wasn't unusual, however,
he gave me an odd look.

"Yes, Jarvis?"

"I beg your pardon, sir?"

"You lost control of an eyebrow, it was slightly raised in a
question. Anything the matter?"

"Sir, if you'll permit me. You seem troubled. In the two
short visits I've made to your room today your attention has
been quite taken with the bureau there," and he pointed, as
if for emphasis.

He was quite right, of course. I had noticed my attention
straying towards that part of the room, but it seemed I had
not properly acknowledged it until it was pointed out to me.

"Hmmm. Thank you, Jarvis. I think I must take a look
into what Lady Proctor brought us. Please secure the
room." I gave him a stern look to reinforce how serious my
instruction was.

"Of course, sir. Will you require any assistance?"

"Thank you, but no. I think this is something that would be safer to investigate alone."

An expression crossed Jarvis' face that I quite clearly read as 'Safer for whom?', and he left. I trusted that he would go through the proper lengths to secure the room fully, not only physically but magically. He wasn't a practitioner, as such, but he'd been around my business long enough to have picked up some very useful titbits.

I felt the pull of the book still. I walked around the space, trying my best to stay away from the bureau as I secured the room from the inside. It was mostly magical containment designed to keep things in, which had a slightly unfortunate byproduct of blocking help from the outside.

Once I was sure I could not be disturbed I sat cross-legged on my rug. I controlled my breathing, closed my eyes and forced myself into a trance. It's always important to clear one's mind when tackling an unknown occult threat.

My breathing was shallow and barely discernible. My heart rate had slowed to a handful of beats per minute, but my mind would not clear. The nagging pull of the book remained. I could not ignore it. The affect was already within me, this was as isolated at I could become. I felt like a knight going into battle knowing a gap in my armour was plain to see.

I placed high candleholders around my reading chair, lit them and burned a sprig of herbs to define a circle around where I would examine the book. All of this was accompanied by the intensifying call of the volume. It was irresistible. I briefly wondered how Lady Proctor had avoided its tempting cry.

I braced myself as I opened the bureau, and a wash of charged atmosphere blasted out as though it had been building in confinement. My hands shot to the book and I grabbed it, clutching it to my chest.

I had to force myself to move back into the room and enter the circle I had marked. The flames of the candles guttered, the light seemed to dim. It was mid afternoon when I had begun my preparations, it couldn't have been dusk yet.

I flopped into the chair, my legs weak from the effort to guide me where I wanted to go, seemingly against the will of the book. I held it in front of me. It was quite unimpressive; a plain green leather binding lightly embossed with a pattern of leaves. There were no other markings. I ran my fingers across it, feeling the texture, enjoying the scent. I smelled morning dew and jasmine.

My fingers found the edge of the cover and I knew I was not fully in control of my actions. I was excited, but I should have been fearful. I spend my life in full control.

There were a few flyleaves, the same pattern from the cover had been inlaid or watermarked into the paper, which was thick and crisp, but pleasantly yielding. The book was a joy to hold, a beautiful object before one even considered its contents.

There was no title. No author. The prose simply began.

The eye soaked up the words, floating across the pages, ravenously consuming the story that had begun.

It was a simple narrative about a gentleman who was not described in detail, but had a familiar feel. He had gone for an evening stroll around the streets of his residence. He nodded to people he knew on sight but had never properly engaged with. He enjoyed the smells and sounds that defined this place as his home; it was comforting. The kind of comfort one only feels in hugely familiar surroundings. It is a bubble of existence that cannot be pricked from the outside. It is closeted and intimate, the only place in the wide world you can strip back your social armour and properly be yourself. Not the self others expect you to be.

Then there was something odd.

An alley between two houses that the gentleman was sure he had never seen before. It was impossible. He had walked those streets for years, knew every building, every brick. He was certain this ginnel was somehow new; a ridiculous thought, as the buildings either side of it were hundreds of years old.

Feeling as though some new danger had sprung upon his world, the man investigated. The passageway was dark but smelled fresh and clear. There was no rubbish or detritus that you would usually expect of such places. The brick walls were sheer either side, and when he looked up he thought they went on forever; there was just a thin strip of sky far, far above. The thought crossed his mind to look behind him, but he didn't. He felt that might somehow be dangerous, plus he was on a mission to make sure his home had not been compromised.

His idea of time slipped away. There was only the path ahead, which had begun to soften; the bricks receded, giving way to bushes and plants then eventually trees, until he was in the middle of a sun-bathed glade. Now was when he decided to look back, only to find no evidence of the path that had brought him to that place.

A mild stab of concern prodded his mind, but his senses were drunk on the wonder and atmosphere of the forest. The ground beneath his feet was firm, but yielded to his step, like a cushion. As his shoes disturbed the grass a fresh scent leapt up, which was invigorating. The light that cascaded through the foliage of the trees was warm and hazy; it softened the edges of his vision, and made everything look just a touch unfocused.

Such was the comforting effect of the place, the man felt relaxed enough to lie down on the cosy mosses in the crook of some tree roots.

Of course, he fell instantly into a deep slumber and dreamed the vivid dreams of the enchanted.

My fingers found the edges of the pages with ease, the action a reflex as the words tugged at my eyes, their meanings ringing clear in my head; the images they described had a crisp clarity. I could not draw my gaze from the page. At times I became totally unaware of my physical body; I felt as though I was actually in the story, experiencing the same thing as the central character.

All the time I had a nagging feeling at the base of my skull that something was off. It was easy to dismiss; I was so overtaken with the narrative.

In the story the man's dreams were strange but wonderful. He met a huge cast of characters among a travelling troupe of entertainers. There were dancers, jugglers, conjurers, clowns, and those that could achieve immense feats of physical prowess. They were all tall and beautiful, androgynous and lithe; their smiles filled him with joy, and their laughter uplifted his spirits.

The man found himself in a crowd, watching the show in a forest clearing that looked very much like the one in which he had laid down to sleep.

It was dark, but glowing lanterns had been strung between the branches casting an ethereal light. Flames leapt up from the ring the performers used as a stage; flames from a central fire they danced around, flames from the batons they juggled, flames from a clown that comically burned its own sleeve.

The crowd roared with laughter; they 'oooohhhhh-ed' and they 'ahhhhhh-ed' in perfect synchronicity. All eyes were locked on the performers.

A sharp pain stung the base of the man's neck, and he was jolted out of sync with the crowd. He winced and cried out, his hand flying to where the pain had struck. The performers froze. All the faces of the crowd turned to him.

Silence.

For a split second, the performers were old and withered; they hissed and leered at him through broken teeth and crooked expressions.

Then everything continued as though nothing had interrupted the show. It was forgotten. But the man had seen. He looked around the crowd, noticed their vacant eyes, heard the hollowness of their voices. Felt how cold their presence was all around him.

The fire at the centre of the ring flared as a conjurer threw powders into it. The crowd whooped. The man was silent. There was no heat coming from the fire.

The man looked to his left. He was next to an elderly lady. Her eyes were fixed on the entertainment, her mouth agape in wonder. To his right sat a young man, barely in his twenties, likewise amazed at the show. Both seemed brighter than the rest of the audience, somehow more substantial.

A trapeze artist swung across the glade, barely missing the flames as they flared from the conjuror's powders. Back and forth, back and forth; it was mesmerising - the speed, the danger.

Again the sharp pain hit. The man mastered his reaction. There was no halt to the show, but he was once again aware, out of sync with the crowd.

Something was wrong.

The tips of the man's fingers had begun to feel a chill. The same went for his toes. It should have been warm in the clearing; the fire was vivid and dancing, but it seemed to the man that it was absorbing heat, not giving it.

The man looked down at his hands. There was a ring on his finger, a seal used to mark letters or official papers. He recognised it. The initials S.P. They were familiar, but he didn't know why. It suddenly felt important to know why, but the fire was inviting, the entertainment alluring. It seemed like a much better idea to simply relax and watch the show.

Another pain flashed down his entire spine. The man jumped to his feet, howling, and he ran from the clearing into the dark forest beyond, leaving the cold light behind and the blank stares of the crowd who had suddenly become faceless ghosts moaning for his return.

As soon as he left the clearing the lights were extinguished and he was in a void.

Silas Pope. S.P. I was the man in the book. I was in this place, or at least a part of me was. The chill still stung my fingers. I feared a part of me would remain there even if I found a way out.

I had been reading a book. Just reading a book.

I rubbed my neck and back. The pain was still there, a protective enchantment to shock me out of an unintended trance. Something I had seeded in my mind long ago upon the instruction of my mentor, something I had never had cause to rely on.

I could not remember falling into the narrative. I did not know how to leave. Looking around in the darkness, I heard noises. Rustling, movement and animal calls.

All stories should have a denouement. An ending. But this one usually didn't. It invited the reader in and kept them entertained until they were drained, keeping its own story alive and never needing to end. A self-sustaining narrative.

I flared a light in my palm. I still had some power in this place. I had regained my wits. I would have to make an ending.

This was an old story, one that had not needed to defend itself for an age. I hoped to find it lazy and unprepared, fat on the spirits of all those it had consumed... every soul in the crowd.

Unfortunately, anything ancient has managed to survive for very good reasons.

A gout of flame erupted above the tree line in front of me. A signal. A challenge.

I walked towards the plumes of fire. Each illumination showed a crowd of spirits following me; the hollow eyed, slack mouthed ghosts that were the past victims of this book. I didn't know if they were herding me to a similar fate, or hoping to see me succeed and be released.

Somehow I had entered the clearing again, even though I was sure I had walked away from it and never changed direction. At the centre sat an enormous dragon. It was a worm of antiquity; a slender scaled body, long limbs and tail, no wings, and a huge snouted head with knives for teeth. A forked tongue flicked out from its mouth, tasting the air, sensing my approach.

I had to take the role of dragon slayer. This truly was an old story.

The ghost crowd surrounded the glade, staying in the trees. Tall shapes stood among them, tall but bent and broken. All of their power used to deceive earlier was now being spent upon the dragon. The true form of the performers revealed a race of beings whose presence I had long suspected in our world but had never seen explicit proof. They were Fae.

I focused power to my hands, still tingling from cold at the extremities. On my left arm I formed a shield, and in my right hand a mighty flaming sword.

I had no hope of slaying a dragon, none at all. But a story needs an ending. It craves it, and this story had not seen a fitting conclusion in centuries.

The dragon spat a small flame towards me. I raised my shield and felt its icy blast. Just a test.

I circled the clearing, keeping my guard. I'm no great swordsman; I prefer the stealth and intimacy of a knife. It was all for show.

I feinted left. The dragon read it, and gnashed its teeth around my standing leg. I felt a snap, and crumpled to the ground. I kept my shield up, flailed my sword and struck a glancing blow to the beast's clawed foot.

To my surprise, the dragon howled. It was barely a touch, but the heat of my power had stung. I became bold and cast aside my weapons.

The worm paused, considered my defiance, and breathed its chill flame to envelop me.

As the cold spread through me, I felt the energy leaving my body. It spread from my hands and feet up my limbs to my torso. I knew if it reached my heart I would become a husk like the rest of them.

The dragon began to howl. The energy it was siphoning from me was hotter than it could bear. It writhed and slithered in coils around itself, the flames of my power erupting from between its scales and returning back to me. The warmth began to beat back the chill as the dragon burned.

The crowd of spirits began to fade. A weak dawn was breaking behind the trees, and the Fae looked upon me with fascination and naked fear.

Once again I formed a sword in my hand, approached the twisting dragon, and in one sure stroke claimed its head.

The beast exploded in a blast of icy flame and threw me out of the clearing, back to my office. My chair had fallen over backwards and I was sprawled behind it, just barely within the circle I had formed.

The book was on the floor, flames crisping and blackening the pages. It crackled and spat, then the cover creaked shut extinguishing the fire and leaving behind a husk of the volume it had once been.

I gingerly approached the book's remains, now simply two covers with a barely connecting spine. It was black on the inside, while unnervingly untouched on the outside. Any power it once had seemed spent.

I kept the remains in the archives. It is the first absolute proof I have of the Fae's existence in this world.

I have heard tell of similar devices made in the underworld. Soul Reapers, passive traps set to steal away innocents. This one was different. It had a similar mechanism, but the energy it took was not a simple prize; I suspect it sustained the place the story had taken me to - whatever that place was.

I was saved not only by my preparations and protections, but also by my unique nature. The book had been feasting on souls for a long time; short lives that burned brightly and briefly. My life force proved too much for it. I do believe I gave it a stomach ache as it attempted to consume me.

It hadn't been expecting to ingest an immortal.

I recount this tale, and I will read it back many times as a reminder. Stories are dangerous; they have a life of their own. The reader cannot trust in the words, cannot rely on the control or skill of the author. Next time you get swept away in a narrative, simply cannot stop turning the pages, and fall into that magical state of fiction, beware. For you are in more danger than it might seem.

Stories will claim a part of your soul. If you aren't strong enough they may take it all.

ᒪᒪᒪᒪᒪᒪᒪᒪ ᒪᒪ

My name is Silas Pope. A kind man called Mr Hopkins has taken me under his wing, and suggested I should try to write about what happened. He gave me a small stone to hold as I do it. Says I'll feel much better afterwards.

I hope he's right.

My hand is shaky and my tears smear the ink. I don't rightly know where to start.

⟨ 𝓑𝓲𝓻𝓵𝓪𝓻𝓮𝓴𝓽 𝓲𝓼 ⟩

Water runs wherever it may. Man has made strides to control it, or at least guide it for our own purposes. But it really is a rule unto itself. It carves its own path; if it meets resistance above ground it goes under to find a new way. It seeps between rocks and soaks through stone.

Water cannot be contained. It has power born of an elemental freedom. Power that one must think twice about before confronting. Power that is difficult to chase.

This is precisely what I was attempting.

It was like chasing a raindrop to the ocean.

However, my raindrop was leaving a heinous trail. A sickness touched the towns and villages near each river the rogue water spirit usurped.

It had all begun at Sunderland with the murder of the Naiad who had previously protected the River Wear. Its blood had contaminated the water, and with no elemental spirit to replace its influence the disease had taken root.

The perpetrator of this terrible crime had moved on, but not before leaving an egg behind in the Wear. It was a rogue Naiad that had been illicitly transported across from the European mainland. It was haughty and ambitious. Not content to make its new home in the river it arrived in, it has continued its search for greater waters.

I tracked her across the north-east of England. She hopped from river to stream, trespassing in tributaries and killing any spirit she found in prominent rivers. Each time leaving an egg in the soiled waters, so one day her daughters will rule a minor realm of their own, while their mother seeks out her bigger prize, safe in the knowledge that she has seeded her influence throughout the waterways of the land.

She headed north, initially, and was rewarded with the strong flow of the River Tyne. By devouring the spirit of the Wear she had regained enough strength to tackle the Tyne Naiad. My investigations rooted out witness testimonies from various water based Elementals (Grindylows, Peg Prowlers, Greenteeth and the like) and by all accounts the intruder was very nearly bested by the spirit of the Tyne. It's not all that surprising, a strong industrial river like that. But the newcomer fought dirty. She has a vicious streak that the resident Naiads have never encountered before. They have become complacent, a little soft.

Again an egg was left in the dirty waters of the Tyne, and the disease was spread to the populace. It began with giddiness, then a sickness of the stomach, cramps, and general agitation. The body purges itself and slowly, ever so slowly the victim of the illness will get weaker until they fade and die. They try to wash them, keep giving them 'clean' water to drink, but it is the very thing that is killing them, it is the thing that is spreading it.

I have tried to advise the authorities as I have chased the Naiad across the north. It seems as though smaller tributaries are relatively safe; their spirits remain intact, the risk of battle too great for such small prizes. It is the large bodies that she desires, and where there are large bodies of water, there are more people.

I've advised that water be brought in from smaller sources, where possible seawater transported is to be distilled. In truth, my warnings have fallen on deaf ears. Everyone believes the illness is spread through 'bad air' and 'sour vapours'. Too little is generally known about how illness travels from person to person. I was there when this began; I know it is the water that has poisoned our land.

I sent urgent messages back to London. I requested that as many agents as we could spare be deployed to major waterways, meet with the river-dwelling communities, and tell them what had happened; warn them what may be coming their way.

It was too late for the Tees, the Ure and the Ouse, as the Naiad struck back south. She had her bearings now. I believed I saw her mind, guessed at her strategy, but I wasn't sure if we could stop her before she built her strength. She was a daughter of the Rhine. The current of power is strong there. I wondered if she would dare to challenge for the Thames?

By the time I had travelled south as far as the River Trent I was rejoined by Special Constable Jenkins. He had made an admirable recovery from our misadventure in Sunderland. As I hoped, he was only short a few fingers, and it seemed his bravery was 'none the worse for Wear' (a terrible joke, I'll admit, but he rather enjoyed it, or at least was polite enough to pretend).

Help from London hadn't made it this far north and I wasn't sure if we had got to the third longest river in the kingdom in time.

I usually find animal sacrifice distasteful, but expediency was vital. It is the quickest way to summon a minor natural deity. I wanted to show deference, but not needlessly waste the life of another creature. I went with a brace of coneys that I had snared for my own dinner. Technically they were already dead, but fresh enough to make my point. I laid the rabbits on the bank partly submerged in the water, and whispered a short but powerful oath as a polite summoning.

We waited an hour with no response. A dark cloud in my mind gathered. I knew we were already too late. I decided it was pointless to stay and gather confirmation. We needed to get ahead of this.

I was lead agent in the field, which gave me a certain level of sway, but my choices would be picked over closely and measured against the results. I looked south-west, there was the Severn away over that horizon, and of course the Thames to the south. I felt that this Naiad would not settle for second best, but would have to drain the power of all the original river spirits to even attempt to take on the Thames.

I realised to be properly prepared for the fight that was to come I would have to sacrifice protection over the other rivers. We would make the last stand at the toughest test.

I had struggled with the pair of rabbits, so I found it slightly unsettling that my choice to condemn thousands of people to death through disease had come so easily.

The only way to save all of the rivers, to replace their spirits with new Naiads, was to protect Thames and ask her to repopulate the waterways of the nation. Only new spirits could cleanse the rivers and remove the sickness.

As we travelled south back to London I was getting reports that confirmed my suspicions. The invading Naiad had headed west, building momentum to take on Severn. All the while I was hoping that each challenge would prove too much, that she might meet her match and be defeated. It pained me to not be more active in the fight and have to rely on the elements. In fairness, their power is beyond me. I couldn't hope to match them on my own, but I could make an excellent ally.

I visited the River Lea at Cheshunt before entering London proper, and made another sacrifice. Jenkins winced when I mentioned it. I doubt he was squeamish; I assumed he considered himself an accidental sacrifice on our previous adventure.

I waited long enough to feel the creep of nervousness. I had taken my boots off, rolled my trousers to my knees and stepped into the waters. I let some of my magical energy into the river. It was like leaving a calling card with a butler to be considered for admission. I also hoped it would amplify my original offering.

I felt Lea approach long before I saw her. The river around us began to clear, as though a light was shining within it. The sound of the flowing water rang clear like silver bells, and a clean natural scent drifted up from the flow in a vapour.

A beautiful figure rose from the depths and broke the surface. She was humanoid in shape, with a few notable embellishments; fully webbed fingers and I've no doubt toes, fins protruding from her forearms, and a large one on her back. She had no need for gills; her appearance was mere window dressing. She appeared to me as I expected to see a water spirit. I thought back to what the Groac'h had told me in Sunderland and had trouble imagining this demigoddess being capable of violence. I decided not to trust my eyes.

I bowed deeply, making sure my head touched the water. "Lady Lea, your humble servant, Silas Pope. Thank you for granting me an audience."

The Naiad smiled. It was like a cloud had moved and unblocked a soft shaft of light. "Mr Pope. It is my pleasure to receive you. Though I believe I have already had word of the news you bring to my currents." Her mouth never moved, I simply heard the words in my head. Her voice was as beautiful as her smile.

"Yes, I'm glad the news has reached you, and that you might be wary of the threat, but my fear is that the invading Naiad will target the Thames herself."

Lea's smile faltered. "She would dare to challenge Mother Thames? Surely not?"

"I believe the intruder is a Rhinedaughter. Proud and haughty. She will settle for nothing less than the greatest water in this land. She has built her power by consuming the spirits of your sisters, and polluting their homes. A sickness has spread and cannot be stymied."

"What do you think I can do to stop her?" It was a genuine question, and I was taken aback that the undeniable power in front of me had already assumed defeat if ever she was challenged.

"If Lady Thames is challenged, I would hope she could prevail. I am here to ask if the daughters of the Thames can rally to her and aid her in battle?"

The smile brightened once again. "You have a good heart, Mr Pope and a keen mind, but you do not know our nature. We cannot leave our dominions, for we are the river. We flow into the Thames, we already lend Mother our power. Even if it were possible to offer our assistance, the Lady Thames would scoff. It is our duty and our right to fight for what we are, what we preserve.

"You have power, Mr Pope. You know its pull, its cost. But you know nothing about being power."

I suddenly felt very small.

The voice in my head gained additional pressure - an urgency. "If you truly wish to help Mother Thames in the fight that is coming, I suggest you ask her yourself, but there's no need for the formalities you've afforded me. Simply set yourself adrift on her tides and commune with the eddy and flow of her. She'll tell you precisely what she needs from you."

I bowed once again, touching my forehead to the river. She disappeared, and it was as though the sun had gone back behind a cloud. I turned towards the bank to see Jenkins looking at me, worry etched across his face.

"No luck, sir? Should I find a larger animal to, erm, offer?" asked Jenkins. It was clear he had not witnessed the meeting.

I patted him on the shoulder, still carrying an enormous sense of bliss as a result of my encounter. "No, Jenkins. I have my orders. When gods speak, not everyone gets to hear it," I shrugged. "Seems rather counter-productive to me."

Gloucester reported a cholera outbreak shortly after. Severn had fallen. The death toll was terrible and that was based on the patchy messages and vague counts from town to town. One had to assume the reality was much worse. The poor were suffering most; they had no way to avoid the tainted water. I had to accept that I was complicit in the massive loss of life. It was a burden I had to carry at the time, and one that not even the power of this Sentiment Stone can fully lift. I received notes from various acquaintances in the know, telling me my sense of responsibility was askew. Likening it to feeling responsible for the deaths wrought by a flood or a drought, as though this was yet another natural force at work that humanity was almost powerless to stem.

They used the word 'almost', which shows that they know a good portion of my character. For there is always something to be done, even if we cannot control its effect. Sometimes the act of doing alone arms us against the onslaught.

Once we were back in London proper I relieved Jenkins of his duties, told him to return to his wife and girls. There was very little he could do to help with the task that needed to be done. I wasn't surprised to hear his refusal, and I was a little pleased. He had been useful and good company on the journey south. I questioned his willingness to fling himself into danger; from my point of view he was as rich as Croesus, he had treasure I could never hope to amass; his family. I knew his mind would not be changed, but I chided my weakness and promised myself that I would do better to protect him this time.

I don't believe in coincidence, but I think life gives us moments of providence. We headed to the docks to find a vessel willing to give me passage down the Thames so I might try to communicate with the river spirit. We met an unlikely ally; Captain Ryba, he of the quarantined ship that we had helped in Sunderland. The very same ship that had unknowingly brought the Rhinedaughter to our shores.

I'd been spotted from the ship, and Ryba sent a crewman along to take me aboard. He grasped my hand in his huge paw and shook it vigorously. "Mr. Pope! I never thought I'd get a chance to thank you properly for the assistance you provided. I know it was you who managed to turn the minds of those quaymasters to let us dock and restock."

I looked around at the crew and saw that they were still recovering from their long quarantine. There were a lot of cinched belts, and not a small amount of loose skin. We got bows, nods, informal salutes and mostly smiles from the men. After weeks of feeling responsible for a great amount of death, it was gratifying to be reminded of the few lives I had managed to preserve.

The captain invited us to his table for a meagre meal. It was all they could scrounge together; even though their lives were saved in the north, their business was in ruins.

I tried to explain what was happening, what I believed needed to be done next. I didn't try to hide behind stories or lies. Ryba deserved the truth, even if he wasn't willing to accept it.

As it turned out he took it all in without blinking, as though it was the most natural thing in the world. His laugh was rich and deep. "My good sir! A life at sea soon shows you the power of nature and gods. If you think to surprise me with your tale, I'd tell you it is the most fitting explanation I've heard for what is happening in this land."

I was glad to hand over a bag of coins for the captain's ship and the service of his crew. Not quite as glad as the captain was to take it. I had warned him of the dangers; the very real, mortal dangers. Ryba accepted them with a wink. I realised that every voyage he undertook ran similar risks to what I would ask of them. One short-term perk of taking the ship into service was that the meals improved instantly.

I asked for the ship to be made ready. I simply wanted them to sail as far down the Thames as they were able, then turn around and come back up to the estuary. If necessary, I requested that they repeat the journey until I had done what I needed to do... I didn't really know what that was at the time.

The crew cleared the bottom cargo hold. I wanted to be as close to the water as I could. In fact the ship was carrying a

47

little water from leaks in the hull, which I thought a perfect condition. I made Jenkins and the crew leave the cargo hold, extinguished all the lights, and let myself float upon the waters of the Thames in total darkness.

It made no difference to my perception if I had my eyes open or closed. The water lapped against me. I couldn't sense the hull of the boat beneath me; it was just the water around my body. I reached out with my senses. With no visual stimulus I had to concentrate on the sounds and smells.

I let the river enter my consciousness.

I didn't converse with Mother Thames. It was more intimate than that. We exchanged thoughts, feelings. Lady Lea was right - I knew nothing about 'being' power. I never would. Never could. But my calling has always been one of serving powers.

I offered my service, and was shown how I might be of assistance.

I'm not used to being shocked.

Mother Thames was very clear that she would fight the battle that was hers, and hers alone. The idea she had for my role was more of a contingency. One I hoped dearly would not be needed.

To make the proper preparations I would need more help… substantial help.

There are areas of London that exist in parallel to 'the norm'. There are communities that dip in and out of dealings with humanity, but go largely unnoticed for who and what they really are. Common folk mostly mistake them as people from 'foreign parts'. They don't give it much thought.

I needed the assistance of the Grindylows.

They are a water people. Their physiology is suited to rivers and seas, but they are in fact amphibious; as comfortable on land as they are submerged. You have to really look to notice them. The gills in their neck are under their jawline, any fins are usually hidden by sleeves, and it's a lot more common to meet folk with webbed hands in London than most would like to admit. Usually they have flat noses and a sallow grey tinge to their skin. They're hairless and have unnervingly sharp teeth that you will only notice if you ever make one smile, which is unlikely.

Of course, they mostly live along the river. By choice they barely touch the land, preferring to stay afloat. They work the river through many trades, and I'm of the belief that without them the city would grind to a halt. They are a major cog in the industrial and commercial machine.

As a senior agent it has become my responsibility to make contacts within all of the 'Elemental' communities (there are many). The Grindylows were one of the more integrated races. They mix with mortals well, even though that means passing for human rather than being up front about their true nature. That isn't an option for most others, as their differences are too marked and obvious. The world is slowly evolving, but I'm not sure when it will be ready to accept the realities of nature's diversity. I fear we will have to wait for mortals to accept one another first. I wonder if it will be within my lifetime?

My contact worked as an estuary pilot. He knew the depths of the Thames better than any other living soul, mostly because he had swam them his entire life. It was his job to board visiting ships and bring them safely into harbour. His job had made him comfortable in human company, and his knowledge had forced humans to look past his odd appearance and accept him through reliance. After years of this he had become gregarious, and was the perfect liaison between mortals and Grindylows.

I arranged for Old Ned to board Captain Ryba's ship as soon as I could. I didn't know any other name for him. He was 'Old Ned' to every single person that knew him. I believed the Grindylows had names in their own language, but they all kept human monikers to blend in when needed.

Ned took the helm of the boat, steering with one hand and puffing on a pipe in the other. His facial expressions gave nothing away as I made my request. I suppose it was more of a business proposition, as I had the strength of the treasury behind me. We would be bankrolling the majority of an entire manufacturing sector for, hopefully, no more than a week. I couldn't be sure how long we needed. If the Rhinedaughter arrived before we could make preparations, Thames would have no contingency.

Old Ned heard me out, said he'd take the plan back to his people and let me know later that day. All very simple and straightforward. No need to negotiate, no smoke and mirrors. They would either help or they wouldn't. For a spy it is rare to deal so cleanly with anyone. It's the only way to deal with the water folk - any hint of deception and they will turn their backs and never let you back in. You get one chance and if you ever default they will never deal with you again. Trust is their currency. I hoped I had built up sufficient credit.

It was a nervous wait, but now I was back in London other concerns began to creep into my days, which seemed absurd with the major threat creeping closer to the city. It was odd being one of only a few people to know the danger, and witness life rolling along obliviously. I had to sift a few prospective recruits; the British Occult Secret Service (BOSS) has always had a... 'unique process' to bring new agents into the fold. There was some trouble from an irritable Indespectus, and there was a tense situation with the Bluecap community with talk of making tunnels underground for public transportation.

These matters diverted me somewhat, and kept at bay any nerves I felt about the answer I would get from the Grindylows. Before dusk a small vessel pulled alongside, and a messenger from Old Ned confirmed their agreement.

They would manufacture and lay the immense amount of copper wire nets I had requested.

What I needed to create was a huge engineering challenge. I was tempted to also ask the Dweorgs, but I needed to keep the circle as small as I possibly could. The Grindylows were expert net weavers. Copper wire was surely an unusual material to use, but I would have never known it. After a few days I was invited by Old Ned to inspect their progress.

We had set up a base of operations at Canvey Island. If we were pushed to enact our plan we would disrupt shipping into the Thames for weeks. If Thames failed in her defence of the river, I didn't know what might happen. I'll admit, I did wonder if the new Naiad did a good enough job that the populace might not notice the switch? If she defeated Thames, perhaps she would claim and cleanse the river for herself? Might it be the beginning of a natural re-balancing?

I cast my mind back to my experience with Mother Thames. She was older than any other entity I'd ever encountered. Surely any change in such a central natural power would unbalance the very essence of our city, our home? I hardened my resolve and concentrated on the job that had been assigned to me.

The nets were ideal and quite beautiful, the craftsmanship stunning on a scale that I couldn't quite grasp. We really had brought an entire race of people to one place to ply their skills and knowledge for a single end. I think that said something special about the Grindylows, how easily they could gather and work in unison.

Strings of boats drifted across the estuary from the shore. They were careful not to block the shipping lanes, and with the pilots being Grindylows there was never any danger of disruption. They also had to be careful not to raise any suspicions as to what we were up to. Nets were not only being made above the water; as the vast sheets were made they were taken underwater, threaded together and laid out for use when the time called for it. As the days passed, more substantial boats appeared along the line that the net ran along the bed of the river. These would be the hoist points. We required large ships, as we needed as much net above the water as below.

The work was completed in twelve days. More than I would have liked, but once I'd witnessed it, the scope of what I had asked seemed inhuman. I suppose it was… perhaps it seemed 'ingrindylow?' The hoist boats were manned around the clock, and Captain Ryba's ship made up the central part of the line.

We had done all we could. Inaction made the waiting even worse. The fear of not being ready in time gave way to the dread of what was inevitably coming.

Of course the Grindylows sensed the change before anyone else. Teams of them were on the riverbed minding the nets, just as teams were on the hoist boats making ready. They reported a tension in the water. I found it difficult to parse that information, but I trusted that this meant the battle would soon commence.

To untrained eyes the battle for the Thames was simply a storm. The kind of storm that convinces you that if the world survives, it will be forever changed for having endured it.

I was stationed on Ryba's ship, so I did not witness the Naiad battle first hand, but I got detailed reports of it from spotters I had set along the length of the river. The Rhinedaughter had approached from the west. She could have entered the Thames where it is small and meanders across England, but she was canny. She knew as soon as she encroached upon any stretch of the Thames that her challenge would be accepted. She hopped watercourses eastwards taking any power she could, spoiling the water as she went, finally feeling bold enough to enter the Thames at Hampton.

Immediately the river rose as though from a massive storm surge out to sea. In reality it came from the west. The water suddenly had to accommodate two enormous sources of power, each vying for supremacy. Water displacement is a very natural reaction; it is the same effect when one gets into a bath.

The pressure in the water began to affect the atmosphere above. Clouds gathered and burst. More water was needed to sustain the forces at play. I had never seen rainfall like it; it came down in sheets. The streets were flooded, buildings washed away into the river, and I dared not think how many lives perished in the deluge.

This was not a physical battle. There were no giant water creatures slashing at one another with claws and teeth. It had all grown far beyond mere physicality. It was an Elemental struggle for dominance; two ancient wills forcing themselves against one another, like powerful magnets that by the laws of physics repel each other, somehow overcoming the rules to clash.

Lightning was forking down from above and always striking the surface of the river, which rose relentlessly. Some spotters would report spectres of huge fish tails beneath the water in the afterimages of the lightning flashes, others said they saw vivid and violent shapes in the spray that rose from the surface of the river with each shattering impact. The fury of the storm travelled eastwards, and a creeping fear began to rise in me. Mother Thames had told me that if she felt the battle was going against her she would bring it towards my position. She would edge it towards the sea.

I saw huge looping arcs in the rainfall. I was convinced they described massive movements of blows in the air above the river.

Nobody was able to fully describe the noise. The thunder struck you dumb, but the squeals and screeches in the air were of no wind I had ever heard. They cut though your body and soul. Made the animal part of your being want to turn tail and run. There was no fight instinct in response to the screams.

As the epicentre of the battle came towards us and passed over us, I looked to shore to see the hundreds of Grindylows that had been stationed below the water emerge upon the shore (a long way inland at this point). The force of the fight had flushed them from their natural habitat. They could not stand the tumult.

Men on Ryba's ship lashed themselves to the masts and railings; these were hardened sailors, men that had ridden the worst of storms and roughest of seas. I saw the fear in their eyes, and recognised its reflection in myself. I'm not accustomed to fear, yet I am unashamed to admit that I pissed myself as the Naiads passed over, under and through our line and out towards the estuary.

As soon as the vile intensity of the battle passed by, the Grindylows (I cannot speak of their bravery highly enough) returned to the water and their posts on the riverbed.

I gave the order to the row of ships to begin hoisting the nets. Thames had told me that if she felt the need to pass my line I must do what we had agreed, no matter what. The fact she had run to the sea was an admission that she was in difficulty. That thought deepened my dread, but sharpened my mind to the task at hand.

The lightning was an unexpected complication. The copper netting rose from the water. It spanned the entire river from Canvey Island across to St Mary's Bay. We had fixed it to the riverbed and hoisted it to the top of the ships' masts. Each time lightning struck the net it would rent holes in it, and bodies would rise from the water. I shouted into the storm for the Grindylows to abandon their posts. The net was affixed; they were only there to see it feed up properly. They needed to get out of harms way. For harm was coming, and it would be by my hand.

I extended a small field around myself, not for protection but to give myself a bubble of quiet and calm. The noise was muted, the squalling winds could not penetrate. Initially it made me uneasy. I felt disconnected from the scenes I was witnessing; men being buffeted by the wind and rain, cowering in fear from the noise. I imagined that this might be what it's like to be a spirit.

The masts of the ships had been rigged with additional spars to thrust the raised netting away from the boats themselves. I had asked for a thick copper cable to be lashed to our mast and lead down to the deck. I had prepared an incantation circle around the mast for the spell I needed to perform. It was simple enough, but I suspected it had never been attempted on this scale before. I was unsure if I had the energy to sustain it, hoping fervently that the copper conduction would make it a little easier.

I centred my mind, grasped the heavy copper cable and began reciting the spell. It was the sort of spell a mentor uses when an apprentice first begins to practice the craft. A simple energy transference. I used to hold an egg in my hand and hard boil it with heat taken from the air around me. In a large open space the temperature transfer was barely noticeable; in a small room, it became decidedly frigid. In this case I was running the spell in the opposite direction. I was drawing heat from the river.

Using the copper netting as a mesh to collect as much heat from the water as possible, I was directing it up, out of the river to be radiated from the copper in the open air.

I could feel it working immediately, the flow of energy from the mighty waters. I merely gave it direction. I herded it, never presuming control. The air around the mesh began to steam and sizzle in the rain, heat flowing from the metal.

The opposite effect was beginning to take hold in the water. I saw icy fingers begin to creep and grow on the river around the places that the net broke the surface.

I wondered how long I could hold the spell in place. How long I would need to freeze the entire span of the river. It was a much bigger task than originally planned, I had not accounted for the floods. I needed to extend the cooling effect beyond the span of the netting we had laid. It would mean more power, more time.

In my bubble of calm the heat was rising. I felt sweat trickling down my back. My eyes were open, but they barely saw what was happening in front of me. All I could see was the energy movement, how it flowed, trying to funnel it where I desired, not through force but by persuasion. Small adjustments here and there to make a path of least resistance, to facilitate a direction that the energy naturally wanted to travel. The conduction of the copper had worked better than I could have hoped. To attempt this spell without it would have been a huge failure. Regardless, my stamina was being tested. I decided I couldn't afford to keep the shield up. I had to compromise my focus for the power needed to maintain my protection.

The noise was like a slap to the head, and the rain once again pounded down upon me. The main difference was the smell - a metallic tang from the heated copper. You could taste its sting on the air. I turned to see if I could spot any signs of the Naiad battle. The intensity of the storm had certainly lessened. I didn't know if that was due to distance, or if the combatants were beginning to tire one another.

I held onto the spell for as long as I could, longer than I should. I looked down the line of ships; a few of them were ablaze. The heat from the netting had caught sail or spar. My direction had not been precise enough. I had stopped the energy flowing down my own connection, but I hadn't kept it far enough from the other ships. The rain helped this problem somewhat, but it all added to the general chaos of the moment.

I looked out to the water. A line of ice went across the river. It had caught a few of the boats; they no longer bobbed or moved, which was unnerving. In fact, I'd only just realised that the sway of our own ship had long since ceased. I tried to spy the far banks to see if we had succeeded in blockading the river flow, but it didn't matter. I was spent. I dropped to my knees and severed the spell.

Nothing really changed. There was no dramatic shift. I had rerouted energy, and the energy continued on its way for a while. It would be days before the ice melted now it was formed.

I passed word to Ryba, I needed confirmation that we had reached both sides of the river. Men began to signal boat to boat using semaphore.

I promptly vomited onto the deck, barely keeping conscious. I hoped we had been successful, but I was conflicted. Our success would mean the death of Mother Thames as well as the Rhinedaughter.

The signal came back. The ice was solid, from bank to bank all the way to the riverbed.

I wept. I didn't know if it was relief or grief. I had done as the river spirit had instructed, and I feared the consequences would be too much to bear. I lay down on the deck, utterly spent. I had no idea what time of day it was. The sky was dark and the storm showed signs of relenting.

The river spirits would be trapped in the estuary, with no way to access the full power of the river. They would weaken and be consumed by the spirits of the sea. The Thames would also be tainted. Naiad blood, if only metaphorically, had been spilled. On top of that, the tainted water had flooded across the city. The sickness would be terrifying.

Now there were no river spirits to put it all right, there was nothing to rebalance the scales. Mother Thames had made it an all or nothing battle.

As I lay exhausted on the deck, my breathing ragged, the rain now gently kissing my face, I felt the death of the Naiads. It was not forceful like an explosion. It sucked at my senses like a vacuum. There was a void in the world.

Just before it hit me, I had a wash of memory, something Mother Thames had planted in my mind for this very moment.

I had further instructions. But they seemed more impossible than the feat I had just achieved. There was one last water spirit in the realm; one that might be able to fix the damage that had been wrought. One that even I had long dismissed as legend.

Her name was Nimue Viviane, the Lady of the Lake.

THE LIGHT OF THE SUBCONTINENT

The heat is tolerable. Its intensity is beyond my prior comprehension, but it is dry. If nothing else it is consistent, which gives you a chance to, if not adjust, at least know what you are in for. However, the light is something I don't believe I'll ever find comfortable. There is a constant glare. It floods everything it touches, exposing the essence, putting truth on show.

I didn't like viewing everything in this light, or the idea of being seen by it.

I'm not certain that it took the unique light of the Indian subcontinent for the commanding officer to take a disliking to me. He made his opinions on my skillset very clear on our initial meeting. He seemed to be a man set upon dismissing anything that he couldn't understand. I might suggest he has turned his nose up at a lot of information that could otherwise have helped him.

In the past I might have wondered how such a man got anywhere near a position of influence or power, but my few short years of training and field experience has shown me the mechanisms of privilege, and the human cost that is ground between its cogs.

Mr Hopkins was acting as senior advisor to General Harris. He had me sent over to Colonel Stuart's company where I was placed with the young, arrogant and extremely ugly Major Dawes. Technically, I was well within my rights to go straight to Colonel Stuart as an advisor, but I felt I was able to be effective in the role I had been given. This was despite Major Dawes' belief that he was placing me 'out of the way'.

I was attached to a light infantry unit; scouts and skirmishers. We went out to get the lie of the land and be an annoyance to any enemies we might find. This suited me just fine. Mr Hopkins has informed me, quite regularly over the years of my apprenticeship, how annoying I can be. Plus it is of great strategic advantage that I can survey the landscape for any occult or magical advantages.

We were around a quarter of the way to Seringapatam in Mysore. It was a two hundred and fifty mile march through the jungle from Madras, and the timing of our arrival was crucial. As you might imagine, it is not a particularly orderly affair, despite the British army or rather the East India Company, being the greatest logistical force in the world. That is to say, the landscape is testing, and it is beneficial to be out front leading the way.

I hadn't had any real need to use my powers beyond the small tricks that impressed the soldiers and established my credentials. It is a huge advantage to be able to light fires easily, especially during rain squalls. Keeping your unit warm and fed with a hot meal ingratiates you to them very quickly. Within days I had become a mascot, of sorts. I was a commodity that they would fiercely protect, simply because I made their lot a bit easier. The life of a soldier is filled with hardships; it takes very little to impress them with small touches of comfort.

I will admit to taking particular pleasure in keeping the rain off of our tents while the rest of the company got soaked.

I made many friends that night, especially Povey and Rider who were on guard, while quite possibly alienating myself from the rest of our detachment.

That small display didn't go unnoticed. There was a suggestion that I might be billeted back with Major Dawes, but I suspected he tripped over his inflated sense of honour and couldn't bear to admit that he had been wrong regarding how useful I could be.

Captain Sage became rather protective when the whiff of losing me floated past. All of a sudden we were sallying further ahead, and spending a lot more time away from the main company.

Sergeant Ottaway had been assigned as my protector. He was a good man, but far too curious about my abilities. I got the sense he saw it as trickery, and wanted to know the secrets behind the 'illusions'.

As our unit got closer to Mysore, around sixty miles, we began drifting back to the company again. The dense jungles were long behind us, and we were marching through rolling hills and farmland. The villages were either abandoned or may as well have been. There was very little to forage and the soldiers were reticent to take shots at wildlife in case an enemy unit was nearby. These suspicions proved accurate.

We were skirting a shallow valley, making sure to keep below the lines of the hills. The shell of a village was in the basin with a trickle of a river running through it. A large outcrop of rock dominated the valley to the north.

Povey had the sharpest eyes and spotted the enemy first. A few were scattered among rocks on the opposite slope to us. They ran as soon as they saw us, disappearing over the brow of the hill. We had no idea how many awaited the report.

Captain Sage ordered us to run for the rocky outcrop, the best defensible position. It was the first time since I h been with the unit that I felt like dead weight. I had delud myself into thinking I had integrated into army life but when a real threat presented itself, the soldiers sho just how far from their level I was. It was an uncomfortable and unfamiliar feeling. I had become used to being the most capable person in any situation in the first few years of my magical tutelage. It's safe to say I had an overinflated sense of my abilities; I was only a boy who knew far too much for my own good.

I ran behind Sergeant Ottaway, across the sloping hill through long dry grass. I almost stumbled a few times over hidden rocks; the soldiers were all sure-footed and confident. They ran stooped, carrying their rifles with an upward slope to ensure their shot remained safely loaded and ready in case they needed it. I don't know how they all managed to travel quicker than me with their hands full. I was unarmed except for a blade that I had taken to carrying, and the magical defences of which I was capable.

I smiled when the captain assigned me a bodyguard. Unbeknownst to the whole unit, I was in fact protecting them all with a weak shield whenever there was a risk of danger. It was too difficult to maintain a wall strong enough to stop a bullet over such a wide area, but I was confident it would slow any projectile enough to render it harmless. If I was in a position to watch the action unfold I could make parts stronger and shift the power at need, but as it was I was doing my best to give everyone a better chance.

Privates' Baptista and Cole were the first to near the rocky outcrop. A puff of smoke appeared over the horizon, followed by a sharp crack. I felt something pass through my shield, and a lead shot bumped gently off of Cole's chest. His hand shot up to check for a wound, and he looked perplexed to find nothing. Meanwhile, Baptista dropped to his knee and returned fire. The rest of the unit overtook them, some pausing to fire, while others overlapped them to gain more ground before firing themselves. The delay was enough that by the time the last man past Baptista had fired, he had been able to reload and continue the overlap. The unit was incredibly well drilled. Their precision and fearlessness as they closed the gap on the hill summit was astonishing. I was told to hang back behind the last man. Ottaway had merged into the movement, and away from me. I was, in fact, approaching him as the last man. He was in the middle of reloading his rifle; he'd just bit his cartridge, the bullet in his mouth, while he poured the powder down the barrel. As he was about to spit the shot into his weapon, a call went up from above.

In all the clamour of gunfire from the unit I hadn't realised that there had been no response. I didn't register that my shield had not been tested beyond that first shot.

We caught up to everyone at the top of the hill. A lone body lay behind the first rocky outcrop. He was an Indian man in a ragged uniform that might have been assembled from a number of different forces. He'd taken a shot of lead to the neck, and was quite dead. Baptista looked down at him, turned his head and spat to the side. Powder burn marked all of the soldiers' faces.

There was no time to linger. The soldiers immediately secured the rest of the summit. They moved quickly and smoothly, checking behind all of the rocks and observing the landscape all around from the vantage. There seemed to be no signs of any other enemy soldiers.

I was at the centre of the hilltop. It was flat, maybe a little concave. Captain Sage was issuing orders for the hill to be secured, and placing guards all around. The unit immediately took care of their own responsibilities, checking and reloading their weapons, making sure they were ready for any other surprises.

Young private Cole, for he was even younger than me, approached once he had seen to his duties. He tugged at his forelock and gave a little bow. "Thanking you, sir. I do believe I'd have come off worse if it weren't for you. Unless that Indian powder is mighty weak I'd have a hole in me," he said.

"Not sure what you mean, Mr Cole." I winked. "Must be terrible powder out this way." He smiled and went back to the other boys, no doubt telling his tale.

The captain and sergeant were having a discussion about the next move. We were all aware that we had been spotted from across the valley by a lookout, and wondered to whom they might have run.

"Just another sentry up here, I suspect," said Ottaway.

"Hmmm, looks that way. Damned odd though. Best vantage for miles around. Why only put one man up here? You'd think it'd be worth defending, wouldn't you?" replied Sage.

I was taking a closer look at our surroundings. The adrenalin of the skirmish was subsiding, my senses equalising. With it came a fresh and unwelcome sensation; a tingle of background magic.

The top of the hill was indeed a small bowl surrounded by rocks. The landscape ran down and away from it in all directions. It was like a lone molar thrust up and out of the gums of the Earth. Debris littered the clearing, bits of wood and twine. The centre was cleared completely of grass, and the dirt looked greasy and ashen. I wandered around the clearing, touching the rocks, laying my ear to the ground and looking through a few of my seeing stones to try and define what I was feeling; I couldn't quite place it.

An unease was growing within me.

"The company are a day behind us. We should probably dig in here and send a runner back. We have no idea what might be coming in response to the alarm, but we can make a good stand here if necessary." Captain Sage was still briefing Sergeant Ottaway.

"Very good, sir," replied Ottaway. "I'll send Hastings, sir. He's the quickest of us. Perhaps Major Dawes will hurry along after us if he thinks there's a chance of glory?"

Sage smirked. "Perhaps indeed, Sergeant." He nodded, and Ottaway left to send Mr Hastings running off back to the company. It would be a long and lonely jog into the increasing gloom and eventual darkness, for dusk was fast approaching.

I was a little tentative at first, but I felt I needed to voice my doubts to the captain. "Sir, I don't believe staying here overnight will be a very good idea."

His brow furrowed. "Mr Pope, this is excellent strategic ground. It would be madness to leave it."

"I realise that, Captain. But I have a strong feeling that we should abandon it. I can't quite say why at the moment. This place is important to that village down there, or at least it used to be. Look at the debris, the soil here in the middle." I stooped to grab a handful of it, and instantly understood. I shuddered.

The captain's eyes widened. "Are you all right, Pope? You've gone white as a sheet. Rider! Over here, bring Mr Pope some water!"

I sat on the ground and private Rider pressed a skin of water into my hand. I gulped it down. "My apologies, Captain, but we most certainly need to move. If we try to stay here after nightfall we will be dead by morning. I'm not sure if I'll be able to protect us."

Rider had a wide-eyed look of superstitious fear. I could read the battle raging in Captain Sage's head, between military propriety and how much he had come to trust my opinion and abilities.

"There's something 'other' at work here?" Sage asked. He refused to use the word 'magic'. I couldn't decide if it was through disbelief, or because he felt the descriptor diminished the things I had done to help them thus far.

I nodded, and to my surprise that was enough.

We decamped down to the valley and the deserted village. It gave us plenty of cover, and was itself the next best defensible position after the hilltop. Once the unit was ensconced, there Ottaway still sent Hastings on his way back to the company. Tensions rose; there were a lot of swift glances and brusque mumblings between the men. They were obviously questioning the captain's sense. Word was passed around that he was acting on my advice, and that seemed to temper the doubt somewhat. I was relieved and humbled by their faith in me, but that was edged with uncertainty.

"I hope, for all our sakes, you're right Mr Pope," he said as we settled down to rest for the first watch. The captain had an almost uncanny ability to read people's thoughts. "But don't fret too much. It's my choice, at the end of it all. You've not steered us wrong so far."

"First time for everything though, isn't there Captain?"

"Don't doubt yourself now, lad." He placed a heavy, calloused hand on my shoulder. "What is that place up there? What do you suspect? I trust you enough to go by your feelings. I'll admit it put the wind up me some too, but I had no reason to think on it."

I filed that comment away for later. It interested me that the captain was so attuned. I swallowed hard. It felt like I was justifying myself to my mentor. I pointed up to the hill, now a darkening jagged shape against the colouring sky behind it. "That's an old, possibly ancient, cremation ground. It's where this village used to burn its dead; lay its people to rest."

"So you were spooked by a graveyard?" Sage seemed doubtful.

"Consecrated ground or places that have cultural significance to the transition of the soul are weaknesses between the planes of existence. They attract some creatures who feed from the energy that leaks either way, but it's never enough to sustain them. They always want more," I replied as ominously as I could.

Private Horry came over to our position. He was stooped and moving as quietly as possible. "Sir, there's movement on the eastern side of the valley, the same direction the lookout ran."

The captain became alert. "Very good, Private. Pass the word - nobody is to engage, unless there's no other choice. We can hope they won't bother with a search in the dark."

Horry scuttled off into the gathering gloom. The humidity of the cooling atmosphere was producing a dusk mist that began to roll across the slopes. The entire unit lay hidden in the dilapidated houses to the north of the village. We all watched at least fifty Indian soldiers march across the valley. They looked as though they were floating through the mist. It was eerie, like an army of ghosts. A small detachment splintered from the main force and headed toward the village.

Sergeant Ottaway nudged me, and nodded his head towards a room deeper in the hut we were hiding. He was preparing for a fight, and wanted me out of the way.

The Indian unit was cautious as they approached. The mist was thinner around the buildings; we could see they held rifles, with sabres in their belts. I strengthened the shield I had put around the huts.

If we were discovered I didn't believe we could escape or survive. Their force was much larger than we expected.

The tension was palpable. I felt it in all of the soldiers. They were ready for a fight; at any moment they would take the initiative, and use the only advantage they had - surprise.

I decided to take a risk.

Dropping the protection, I focussed my power into a new shape. I had to guess the distances involved, and try my hardest to recall the geography. The general direction would be right, but to work effectively I needed to hit the rocky outcrop of the burial ground. Doing any sort of magic at a distance is fraught with difficulty, but what I needed to produce was relatively simple.

I set off a single small explosion on the hilltop. A pause, followed by a group of ten or fifteen similar cracks. I wanted to try to simulate a mistaken shot followed by a small volley of rifle fire.

The effect was immediate.

Shouts and whistles came from the Indian main force. The unit approaching the village turned back to rejoin them. They had a defined target. If the hill was properly fortified they knew they would be in for a bloody fight. The Indians split their numbers to attack the hill on multiple fronts.

Ottaway crawled into the room I was in. He looked rather angry. "Tell me that was you."

I nodded.

"Bloody hell. What do you think you're doing? I have to go tell the captain." He left, cautiously making his way to Sage's position.

Horry was sent back to fetch me. The bulk of the unit had congregated in the largest hut. A few were still watching the Indians attack the hill. They were giving it their very best; rifles cracking as they charged the position, voices raised in fear and anger.

Captain Sage looked furious. "You've gone too far, Mr Pope. It wasn't your decision to make."

I quailed inside. It felt like the first time I had let the captain down. "I made a choice that I felt would be best for us all. If they had found us, there was no way we could have prevailed, and there is nowhere to run." My voice cracked a few times in a somewhat unmanly fashion, but I felt I gave a decent account of my actions.

Sage struggled with his emotions. "It's too late now, we have to deal with what you've wrought. We're still in the same position. What do you think they'll do once they find nothing up there? We can't try to escape - we'll be spotted. There's not a cloud in the damn sky, and the moon is bright." He was thinking out loud. This was a trait in the captain I admired hugely. He never gave the impression he had all the answers, and was always open to suggestions.

I put my hand up timidly. "Actually, sir…"

Sage sighed. "Well, you got us into this. What?"

"We need to try and keep them up on the hill. If my guess is right, they won't be a problem come the morning."

The captain frowned. "You talk in riddles, Mr Pope. You gonna magic them away for us?"

"No, sir… I think there's something up there that will kill them for us. It's why I didn't believe it was safe for us to stay there." The silence after I finished speaking was punctuated by the brave attack on an empty hill by the Indians. "What's the best way to keep the enemy on that hill once they take it?"

Sergeant Ottaway gave a rueful smile. "Sounds bloody silly, sir, but the best way to make an enemy defend a highly defensible position is to…"

"Attack. Yes," finished Sage. "And it is bloody stupid. I'll not risk you all for a bit of theatre."

I nervously cleared my throat. "If you can get me close enough, I think I can put on a show for you."

Ottaway, Rider and Cole escorted me out of the village and up the opposite side of the valley. Although distance made it harder, a clear line of sight took a lot of the guesswork out. We tried our best to find a small hollow or a rock to hide behind, but we had to make do with the long grass. The soldiers had stripped back their gear to a bare minimum, and wrapped as much as they could of anything metal they had on them, to reduce the risk of the light catching us out.

Timing was everything. We formulated our plan and put it into action quickly; we were in position by the time the

Indian attack had fizzled out with the realisation that they were attacking an empty position. The sounds began to quell, but from my vantage they were no less professional than we had been earlier; they scouted around the hilltop, placed guards and generally made it defensible. By that time it was as dark as the night would likely get.

I heard raised voices drifting across the valley, and then around a quarter of the men began to march back down into the valley towards the village. I suspected that some of the men had similar feelings to my own about the place and didn't want to stay. But I needed to drive them back.

I'd only spent a few weeks around the army, but I had been observant. Mr Hopkins had advised me before he left for his own post what might be expected of me; useful tactics I might need to employ. I had not been idle. I had practised as well as I could, but I had never attempted anything on this scale.

The darkness would help. It might cover some of my inconsistencies and inadequacies.

I started with a few shouts, and running feet. I added some glints of light in the distance, and the shuffle of men moving with a few barked orders here and there. The whole effect was set off by the first volley of gunfire. Sparks broke the darkness, and cracks rent the air.

I had begun it all from the south end of the valley. To cut off the Indian soldiers approaching the village, I also mimicked shots coming from cover there... once I began, I noticed a few real ones adding to the cacophony. Captain Sage had read the situation wonderfully.

Of course it was all for show. Cheap tricks. A ventriloquist act on a large scale, with a few pretty lights to sell it.

Admittedly, these are very simple effects to produce, but on the scale and co-ordination required to make it believable I was tested to my limits. I had fallen into a trance, seeing not what was in front of me, but the spectrum of magic at play overlaid on the physical world. I wish I could have shown it to the soldiers, as it had a beauty of its own.

The Indian soldiers approaching the village retreated to the hill. A few of them fell to the real shots from the remainder of our unit. They may have been the fortunate ones.

Captain Sage told me that a full assault of a defended hill would be madness in the dark. If a real company had arrived at that point they would simply have set a guard around the position to wait for morning. I tried to make a good show of it. There were a few shots from the Indians on the hill. I did my best to judge the effects on the far side of the hill to keep the enemy hemmed in.

Then an uneasy peace descended. My work was no simpler; I had to keep the status quo, and create the impression of a large force of fighting men surrounding the hill, waiting for morning to launch their assault. An assault I was fairly certain would not be needed.

Cole heard it first. "Shouts, sir. From the hilltop."

"We have our job, we stay here," replied the Sergeant.

The private wasn't wrong though. There were blasts of gunfire, then more shouts, which turned to screams. A strange light blossomed from the rocky ring on the hill. It burned like a flame, licking a sickly light down the surrounding slopes.

I stopped what I was doing. It wasn't needed any longer. Sweat beaded my brow, and I fell back into a stupor, utterly spent.

I awoke back in the village to the smell of cooking. The unit was around me, and in generally jovial spirits. I could see a simple guard set around the remains of the village. The mood seemed to be one of safety, at least as close as soldiers ever get to it.

"He's up, sir!" I heard a voice that I recognised as Horry's, followed by the sure step of Captain Sage. He stopped and squatted next to me.

"Mr Pope. Glad to see you're back with us. It's safe to say we have a few questions."

I trapped the captain's arm. A horrible thought had occurred to me. "Has anyone gone up to the hill? Tell me you haven't sent anyone up there?" I pleaded.

"Settle back, calm down. I've done nothing. In fact, I told everyone to stay away. After that little show last night we couldn't decide if it was down to you, or something else. We've been keeping a careful watch, but thought it best if we heard your side first."

I sagged back in relief. "Thank goodness. I can assure you, Captain, my efforts last night were purely cosmetic. The flames on the hill were down to something else entirely. Have you seen any survivors?" I asked.

Sage took a moment, sniffed. "A few of them ran from the hill and headed our way. We had no choice but to shoot. They were crazed with fear. We've set a watch the whole night and nothing's moved since that bizarre light faded away. We've been catching a bit of noise on the wind, but nothing substantial, like an animal rooting around or something."

"I doubt very much if there are any survivors. I wouldn't suggest going up to check either. It might be best to leave this place as soon as we might," I said.

"My thinking exactly. When you're ready Mr Pope, we will go back to meet the company. They should be coming up on us by noon."

I looked around. "Where's Sergeant Ottaway? I no doubt have him to thank for getting me back here in one piece."

"He's just doing the rounds of the guard positions, he'll be back shortly," replied Sage.

"Actually, sir, I passed him heading east. Told me he was off to relieve himself, but that was a while ago now," commented Horry.

"Aww, shit," spat Sage.

I was up and running before anyone else could react. The soldiers had no hope of catching me. They shouted for me to stop, to wait. I couldn't. Fear ate away at my gut. "Stay back, don't climb this hill!" I shouted over my shoulder. I heard Captain Sage confirm my request as an order.

My feet were sure and swift, the air in my lungs burning as I ascended the hill. I grabbed rocks and scrabbled up as fast as I could. The ground itself was hot even though the sun was low and still weak. Ash floated in the air with the acrid stench of decay.

I bowled over the lip of the hilltop, raising a strong shield in front of me. I wasn't certain what I would find, but I had a terrible suspicion.

In the dawn light the cauldron of the summit was charred black. A few broken bodies lay around the edges; they were less numerous towards the centre. Fragments of bone, and baked discs of metal that used to be blades spiked the dirt. In the middle of it all, a creature had its back to me, making slurping, crunching noises as it busily devoured a fresh body. Its meal was silent.

Keeping my nerve and shield strong I paced slowly around the stone ring. Upon closer inspection, the monster looked a lot more human than I would have liked. It had long, thin limbs, claws on its hands, and tiger-like teeth that ripped the flesh in front of it with ease. If this wasn't strange enough, it was floating above the ground with its feet pointed backwards.

Before it, ripped in two, was Sergeant Ottaway. He was still alive, if you could call it so. His eyes saw what was devouring him, though belief seemed far away. His vision slipped across to me. His mouth gaped open, but no sound escaped.

The beast's head bobbed down again, tearing flesh and entrails from its prey. Ottaway's hand gripped the ground, clawed the earth, breaking through the black soot and grey embers to the rich dark-red soil beneath. His hand clawed and clawed, his eyes staring at me in desperation.

In an act of pure will, the sergeant grabbed a clod of earth, real earth, and threw it at the creature above him. It struck the monster in its chest; a piercing cry rang out to the sky as though it had been burned, and it fled backwards away from the meal that had fought back.

I dived across to Ottaway and decapitated him with my knife. I sawed away at his neck until I was absolutely certain of his death... of his release.

The creature rose above me, snarling. The earth had stained its white robes. In the strengthening light I realised I could see the landscape through it.

A spirit, then.

It was clear I was being sized up as the next course. I dropped to the ground and began digging. I gouged at the ground with my hands, through the soot, blood, ash, and all kinds of debris I didn't want to think about. I raised the handfuls of red dirt and, rubbed it over my face, up my arms, across my clothes. I tried to coat as much of myself with it as I could. Then I walked towards the ghost.

It snarled, its backwards feet still hovering above the earth it couldn't bear. I thrust my muddy hands towards it, and it moved quicker than my perception, away and to the side.

I whipped around, trying to keep it in front of me. Slowly I backed away towards the edge of the hill, where I'd entered the ring. As soon as I was over the lip I sprinted back down towards the soldiers that waited for me.

I told Captain Sage that Sergeant Ottaway had been lost in the same manner as the enemy. The unit took a moment to mourn together, and then got back to the matter at hand. Soldiers really are a remarkable breed.

We marched back to meet the company later that day, and planned a course onwards towards Seringapatam, avoiding that valley.

We are now in position just outside our destination, laying siege to the city. I've been told a breach has been planned and an attack will be forced any day now. If we can win this day it could be the end of this minor insurrection. It is the first chance I've had to write an account of what I saw during the march. I had an opportunity to consult Mr Hopkins, as we were reunited when the forces converged.

What we encountered is locally known as a Bhoot; a vengeful sprit that cannot move on past its former life. Our best guess is that many years ago, possibly centuries, bodies were cremated at that funeral ground without the proper rights, dooming the dead to a half-life here, and not being allowed to rest or move on. Over time the cremation grounds have been seeded with blood offerings, consumed by the Bhoot that is trapped there. It has become dependant upon its feed. When the village was abandoned due to the war, the Bhoot no longer received its offering. It hungered, became restless. Became bold.

Being stuck between our world and the next, it cannot bear the basic elements of either. Soil and water burned it like acid.

I often think about Sergeant Ottaway. He is my reminder that I must either satisfy or deflect curiosity. I blame myself for his death. I should not have treated him or all the other soldiers as children, too innocent to be fully informed of the dangers.

For some children it is never enough to be told they should avoid the fire because it is hot... they need to experience a burn before the lesson is learned.

Sadly, magic does not scald. It immolates.

ᒐᕑᔑᖾᐣᕕᖾᕕᓇᓇᕕ ᔑᕕ

I'll try again. Mr Hopkins reckons I should write a bit about myself to begin with. Build up to the difficult parts. That's fine with me.

My dad always used to say I had humble beginnings. Especially after I started showing I could do and learn things beyond what he understood. Dad worked as a carpenter's mate. Never managed to put enough by to start anything for himself. I know he was proud to be doing something that just about managed to see Mum and me right.

Mum always told me I was an unexpected miracle. Seems they had given up hope of a family, then I sprang out of nowhere. I suppose it's easy enough to see why they spoiled me, as best they could. Mum was with me every minute I was awake, when I was a boy. Never seemed to tire of me. I'd often catch her just staring at me as though she couldn't believe I was there in front of her. She'd always brush a hand through my hair, or give my arm a squeeze - as much to reassure herself I was flesh and blood, as it was a show of affection.

Dad worked hard to give me anything I possibly wanted. I taught myself letters and reading from scraps of newspaper and books that I found. As soon as I could read and write I always wanted books. My parents never got the hang of it, though I tried hard to teach them. I never thought much of it. But as I got older I realised how lucky I was that they never tried to stop me. I saw it enough - parents determined that their children would not outdo them in any way; that they would be exact copies, doomed to live the same life again.

My mum and dad couldn't really encourage me, as such, but they never tried to limit me either. They really did everything they could.

They were wonderful--

ⵙⵀ ⵥⵙⵟⵥⵑ ⵜ ⵟⵑⵏⵟⵐⵦ

There are valuable items that require additional security concerns. Wealthy people soon learn there are supernatural means to protect their possessions.

Extremely wealthy people need occult practitioners to advise the best way to protect their magical valuables.

It is more of a side-concern for the Service, but a very lucrative one; it accrues funds, connections and information. Spying, after all, concerns currencies of all kinds.

I had been personally responsible for the protective enchantments around the Crown Jewels for a decade or so, when a perplexing case was brought to me.

It was rare for the local constabulary to approach us. We usually informed them that our expertise was needed in their affairs, as it's easier for us to discern supernatural evidence; our mediums tend to point us in the direction of any major spiritual activity. It is common knowledge that the detectives wonder how we get to their crime scenes first. Some secrets are more fun to keep than others.

It clearly galled Detective Hailwood to seek me out, but I knew the situation would have to be desperate for him to do so.

In the end I was glad that he did, even though it caused me a great deal of embarrassment, for I got to meet a thief with singular talents and powers that might yet become useful in the future. I've solved many 'locked room mysteries' in the past, but logic and magic have always dictated that people simply cannot walk through walls… until now.

But I'm getting ahead of myself.

Detective Hailwood was handling a high profile, yet completely secret robbery. Some things are so precious that even if they are stolen, the fact cannot be admitted, especially if the people they were stolen from should not have been in possession of said precious item. The 'victim' in question shall remain nameless, but they were a close acquaintance of the detective. His enquiries were strictly 'off the books' and he requested similar discretion from me, and me only. He wasn't interested in any aid the Service could give, and clearly didn't realise that by this point the Service and myself were quite indistinguishable.

Of course, I needed rather more incentive than common professional courtesy. Luckily, he gave me two excellent reasons that snared my interest. First, the description of the stolen goods; a brown polished stone inside an ornately crafted silver encasement. Secondly, there was no physical evidence that a theft had taken place. It was as if the stone had simply vanished from inside the safe in which it was kept.

Who could resist a puzzle and a treasure hunt?

I cleared my afternoon and met Detective Hailwood at Grosvenor Square. It was an amiable stroll through Mayfair from the headquarters on St James Street. The address alone narrowed down the number of people this secretive client could be. It certainly defined just how rich and influential they could be (it never hurts to make friends in high places, especially when you meet them in low places).

The detective looked uncomfortable as he waited for me to arrive. though few would have noticed the difference in his manner. A slight man, wiry and sharp, he wore a well-tended beard, and dressed above his role as a detective with high end tailoring and dandy flourishes. He came to meet me, moving in a series of jerks and jolts strung fluidly together. I noticed that he had been worrying at some loose skin he had picked around his fingernails, a sure sign that he was tense. It would have been more usual for him to have entered the property and awaited my arrival from within. I wondered what made him break propriety. The owner of the residence rarely enjoys an officer of the law lurking outside. A few small details that I filed away, to see if they would grab any pertinence.

"Mr Pope, thank you for coming. I appreciate your time and attention," said Hailwood in greeting. "I apologise for meeting you in the street, but I'm on instructions. My client will not admit any unknown persons without accompaniment. He has become quite paranoid since the incident."

I stifled my surprise. Whatever had happened was more embarrassing to the client than loiterers. For a Grosvenor Square resident that was quite something.

I presented my card to the butler when we were admitted. We were made to wait for a few minutes. He returned, the master of the house seemingly satisfied, though unwilling to emerge for a meeting. "Detective Hailwood, you have leave to make your investigations, with the help of your acquaintance. I've been asked to remind you of your promise of discretion and sensitivity. If you need my assistance, please call," said the butler, before leaving us to our task.

Hailwood knew the layout of the residence, or at the very least was confident in finding his way to where the alleged crime had taken place. The interior was suitably garish and ostentatious. Once you have seen the inside of one palace they tend to blend together or pale in comparison. I've always found you can tell very little about a person by seeing how they spend their money. You can tell a great deal more by finding out how they accumulated it.

It took a long time to reach the desired location within the twisting halls. I had opened my senses wide since crossing the threshold, and had yet to detect that something supernatural might be present. The only thing that scared me at all were the hideous portraits glaring from the walls. I guessed the branches of the family tree might have been rather thin.

"This is the room in question, Mr Pope," said Hailwood, stopping outside a door that looked like one of the many we had passed on the way. The detective had remained silent on our trek.

We entered a small private library. Shelves lined each wall, floor to ceiling. In the centre of the room there was a grandiose desk and one comfortable-looking armchair with a side table. Nothing about the furniture suggested this room was designed to accommodate more than a single person at a time. There were three breaks in the stacks of books; a large window on the wall opposite the door, a small fire grate to the left, and to the right a section of shelves had swung open to reveal a compartment containing a safe, which was also unsecured. The window looked out of the front of the building with a view over the square. My spatial awareness has always been quite sharp, so the view was what I expected to see, regardless of the long and winding path to the room.

"This door is usually kept locked at all times. The only key is held by the master of the house. This is his personal library, where he keeps some very special and private objects.

Those have now been removed. Oddly, only one thing was taken," said Hailwood as I walked slowly around the space.

"How can I be of any help if the crime scene has been tampered with?" I asked.

The detective looked a little ashamed. "This isn't an official case. I advised the client to leave everything as it was, but they insisted upon removing the other precious items, at the very least."

"How precious could they possibly be? A thief turned their nose up at them," I said.

"The master believes them to be quite important."

"Quite?"

"Only the master of the house and ourselves have set foot in this room since the crime. It is the best that could be managed under the circumstances. It was my hope you may have more unorthodox methods of detection that might not rely on purely physical evidence."

"Hmmmm. We'll see. It is foolish to ignore the obvious. There is rarely a need to strike a pin-nail home with a sledgehammer," I replied.

In truth there was very little to be observed. I inspected the three possible entry points. The door seemed solid enough; the lock appeared strong and untampered. If the thief had got in, it was with the key. The window was similarly unremarkable, its only oddity was the low quality of the glass panes; I could even discern a slight scent from the gardens across the road. The stiffness of the latches was evidence that the windows had not been opened recently. As for the fireplace, it would be difficult for a child to gain ingress, especially without leaving telltale signs. There was no soot or dirt anywhere.

The safe was impressive; thick plate and intimidating cantilever bolts. Again, there seemed to be no obvious signs of foul play. It was simply open as though the combination had been entered.

"Can we be quite sure your client is not mistaken in some way?" I enquired.

"I cannot see any profit for them in how this affair has played out thus far. They haven't officially reported the crime, claiming it as far too sensitive an issue to become public. I'm not entirely certain what the stolen goods are!" exclaimed Hailwood.

"I have a fair guess. If correct, then it most certainly shouldn't be in private hands. In fact, they would have wanted me to stay away from the situation if they were trying to cover anything up. However, if I were to recover the artefact, I might be forced to confiscate it."

"Perhaps they are willing to take that risk?"

"So it would seem. Discounting any fraud, this would seem to be quite the puzzle. Are you willing to leave me alone in this room so that I might make deeper investigations?"

"Certainly, sir. I shall wait outside to make sure you aren't disturbed."

Once alone I climbed onto the desk. Standing tall I had a commanding view of the space. The ceilings were at least twice my height. Every sound was muffled by the insulation of the books. It was a cosy setting. Bearing in mind the previous contents of the safe, I was tempted to browse the stacks to see if there were any occult tomes that might be missing in the BOSS archives.

I reached into my pocket and rummaged through its contents, considering which of my many stones might be of most use. The hag-stone seemed like overkill - I'd work up to that. I considered the moonstone, even the jade, but decided to try the opal. My opal stone was a particularly beautiful specimen; solid black with garish seams of colour, highly polished to be reflective.

Holding the stone to the bridge of my nose and closing my left eye, I looked hard to my right, forcing the very edge of my vision to pick up any sight or light from the opal. In this manner I slowly turned a full circle.

I spotted signs of magical residue in two places inside the room. I was not surprised, though it was comforting to confirm a sensible mechanism for the crime.

I had suspicions about what I was dealing with, but I'd only ever heard rumours.

Upon informing Hailwood that I would accept the case and be in touch with developments, I took my leave.

- - - - - - -

Secrets are quite strange. If they are kept from you it's impossible to comprehend that particular reality. However, when you are privy to a particular secret, you tend to know the ins and outs of it thoroughly. If that secret is the existence of magic in the world, you belong to a select circle of society; a circle that ignores wealth and privilege, concerning itself with knowledge and true power. Sadly, the wealthy and privileged have natural shortcuts to these abilities and information. No matter. If you know, you know, and you are accepted as part of a delicate network. Delicate, but highly conductive - news travels swiftly.

Luckily, so does misinformation.

I used my contacts to seed the story that a security test I set up had failed, the decoy artefact stolen successfully. I was now in need of someone to make a further attempt against the improved measures. I emphasised my confidence by commenting that the genuine article was now in place.

There are brokers for these sorts of things. I made a promise of payment and requested simply to know that the contract had been taken; I wanted to be surprised. There were a number of interested parties. I hoped that the original thief would be tempted back in the belief that they had captured a fake. If not the thief, I imagined news of a fake bezoar on the market would have anyone that had recently acquired one think twice about its provenance. The risks involved to test one are deadly.

I spent the next week at the house on Grosvenor Square. I was made very comfortable, though remained detached from the running of the house itself. I worked from the library room in question and was afforded the one and only key. I slept in the armchair when needed; it was rather tiresome.

There were three dismal attempts to gain entry to the room from various quarters, which involved the use of lesser magics, a mix of confidence trickery, and hypnotism. They got into the house, but never near the room itself.

I knew precisely what I was waiting for. It was much like fishing; a long wait for a fully expected outcome, with the thrill of that event occurring enhanced by anticipation.

The climb was very well done. I wasn't aware the break-in was happening until a foot began to come through the window. You must understand my meaning here. The window wasn't open in any way.

The lightly booted foot was followed by a trouser-clad leg, then a gloved hand, and eventually an entire cloaked body and hooded head. Dressed entirely in black, the figure moved silently across the room.

You may ask how I wasn't immediately detected. I have my own methods of concealment. Shadows have always been my friend and ally.

I noticed the thief moved gracefully, and was of small frame and stature. They were on guard and cautious, obviously on the lookout for the enhanced security measures. They glided over to the shelf compartment, opened it, and then crouched down to the safe.

It was curious to watch as the thief's hands entered the metal door as though it was molten and liquid. There was a slight ripple of distortion around the entry point, but otherwise there seemed to be no visible effect. I was sorely tempted to watch through one of my seeing stones to get a better idea of the magic being used, but I didn't want to spoil the show.

The thief arranged the lock tumblers by feel, extracted their hands, and opened the door. The metal of the safe had reformed perfectly.

Via Detective Hailwood I had requested that all of the items previously in the safe be returned. I gather there was extreme reluctance on the client's part, but I made ample assurances and promises. It seemed they knew enough about me and my dealings to extend enough trust in my judgement. Then again, the emblem of the crown on one's calling card is always favourable.

I had sourced a decoy bezoar. It was simple enough. There are many fakes and curiosities in this line. It was actually more difficult to find a matching encasement.

Deftly, the thief produced a small parcel of cloth from their cloak, unwrapped the genuine article, and swapped it for the replacement.

Before they closed the safe I dropped my own concealment and struck a light in my hand. "That might be one of the more remarkable powers I've had the privilege to witness, and that is quite a commendation."

The thief tensed, their head turned to the window. I imagined they would try to flee.

"If I wanted to arrest you I would have done so as soon as you entered. No, I wanted to speak with you." I gestured to the chair behind the desk. We would be able to speak well enough, even if the furniture wasn't configured for a formal audience. "Please take a seat. My name is Silas Pope, I represent an agency that takes an interest in all things magical on behalf of the Queen."

The thief silently walked across the room and took a seat, though they refused to relax. They perched, ready for action.

I lit the lamp on the desk and extinguished my own light. "You know who I am and whom I represent. May I be furnished with your name, Miss..?"

"You can call me 'Shade'." The thief pulled back their hood. Of course it was a young lady. She had short wavy hair, grey penetrating eyes, a broad nose, and a delicate jawline that softened her other hard features.

"Shade? Very apt, I'm sure. I don't pretend to understand your power, but I've put up a containment field around this room. Partly because I don't want to be disturbed, but mostly to find out if you can escape it at some point." I got up and retrieved the bezoar from the safe.

Shade sighed and seemed to relax a little. Her back sagged, and she sank into the chair. "I knew it was too easy. If you're not taking me in, what do you want with me? If I don't have the goods to take back to my employer I may well be better off in chokey."

"What prison could hold you, I wonder?" She smiled at that. "Do you know what it is you were hired to attain?" I asked.

"I know what it's called and what it looks like. All of which was less important to me than the price offered," Shade replied.

"Hmmm. Bezoars are stones that form in the digestive tract of animals, and sometimes humans; indigestible matter and hair collects and forms into a stone. Once removed they are shaped and polished into this sort of finish." I studied the mottled brown shaded contours on the surface of the stone. It had an off-kilter beauty. "They have a long and storied history. There is a belief that they are a 'cure-all' or at the very least a 'purifier', able to counter any poison. Great kings of antiquity used to employ them as protection from anyone that wished to tamper with their food and drink."

I placed the bezoar on the desk next to two glasses, and a few small bottles I had put there in readiness. "May I have the other stone?" I requested.

The thief placed the cloth-wrapped item on the desk next to its twin. I opened the cloth and each of the silver cases. I removed my jacket, laying it upon the desk, folded my cuffs up with the theatricality of a cheap illusionist, and held up a stone in each hand. I moved them back and forth, and using a simple sleight made them seem to disappear, then reappear. I kept shifting their positions, mixing them and confusing the eye. "I wonder if you can tell the difference?"

A look of abject disappointment clouded Shade's face. "I just returned the genuine article, didn't I?" She cursed. "I knew it! I told them this was a trick."

"Doubled the price, did they?"

A sly smile cracked her visage. "Tripled actually, but I like that you know my mind."

"The real bezoar, in this case, is quite valuable… unique, in fact. It is the only one I have ever heard tell of. This one…" I swapped the stones between my fingers. "Or this one, was formed in the stomach of a particularly powerful magical practitioner. It actually works."

I poured a measure of liquor into each of the glasses on the desk, and then added a few drops from the smaller bottle. Each drop fizzed slightly as it fell. "There is only one true test of a bezoar. One that your employer might have been reticent to try." I dropped a stone into each of the glasses. "Do you know which is the real bezoar?"

Shade shifted in her seat, as though it were suddenly uncomfortable. "I have a good guess."

"Good enough to risk your life? If you choose correctly I'll let you take the stone to your employer, and I'll replace the copy in the safe. My client will never know, if the quality of the rest of his collection is anything to go by."

Doubt clouded her face.

"If you choose to leave both of the stones here with me, you are free to go. In exchange, you'll answer a few questions and be in my debt. There will be a time when I can find a use for your singular talents."

The internal struggle was scrawled across Shade's features. It was clear the idea of being in anyone's debt was unnatural to her, but logic fought hard. "Deal. I've no desire to risk my life for my employer. Can I at least keep one of the cases?"

I pushed the replica case over the desk towards her. "With my compliments. I can suggest a contact that will furnish you with a suitable proxy."

"I'll manage, thank you." She secreted the case in her cloak. "Your questions?"

I settled back into the armchair, selected one of the glasses, and took a long sip. "Why the window? If you can walk through solid matter, why not the walls? It was the only clue you left behind. Actually, that's not quite correct; I picked up on a slight floral scent. I thought it might be from the garden in the square, but I went over to confirm, and realised what I had sensed was in fact a trace of perfume. The more telling clue was the mottling in the glass. When you pass through them they don't properly reform. Certainly not as perfectly as the metal of the safe."

"Very good, Mr Pope," Shade replied. "Yes, I am able to walk through walls, but it has risks and challenges that must be weighed and measured to the situation. Density, thickness, composition - all factors that affect how well I can phase. Windows have a few advantages; it is a material that has already changed form, which makes a difference somehow, and I can see where I'm travelling, which has distinct advantages."

"Quite. Very practical. Can I assume this is a latent ability, and not some sort of spell or enchantment?" I asked.

"Yes, I've always been this way. It was something I discovered as a girl, and came to terms with over time. It has its advantages, and like all power, its drawbacks."

"Care to share those?"

"In your line of work is it common practice to broadcast your weaknesses?"

"If I had any, I imagine I'd be reticent to share them," I smiled.

Shade got to her feet. She moved smoothly, her actions fluid. She placed one hand on my jacket and leaned across the desk, offering her other. "Are we done, then? I have other business to attend to."

I got up, lifted the second glass from the desk and drained its contents, then shook the proffered hand. Her skin was soft, but the grip was like steel.

"Another trick? There was no need to prove you outsmarted me, Mr Pope," said Shade, slightly affronted.

I passed her the small vial of poison. "Feel free to test it. I'll let you decide what is real. Perhaps both bezoars work? Maybe the poison isn't real, or perhaps I can't be killed in that manner? In my line of work, hiding one's strengths is just as important as masking weakness. It might be something to consider, if your career is to progress."

Shade took the vial, a look of mild confusion on her face. "It was interesting to meet you, Mr Pope. I look forward to crossing your path again."

I unrolled my cuffs, put my jacket back on, and gave a slight bow. "The pleasure was all mine."

Shade headed towards the window, but stopped short of it, as though walking into an invisible wall.

"Interesting," I commented. I waved my hand, dismissing the containment.

Shade shot a displeased look towards me, pulled her hood back over her head, and climbed back through the window to find the rope she had used to descend from the roof.

When she was halfway through I put my hand in my pocket for one of my seeing stones, curious to see how the power manifested in a different spectrum.

My pocket was empty, the stones gone.

Shade smiled at me from the other side of the window, gave a little wave, and disappeared from sight.

It never hurts to be reminded of one's humility, but it took me a long time to replace those stones.

& 𝕭𝖎𝖓𝖆𝖗𝖘𝖊𝖊𝖊 𝖎𝖎

There are not many attractive reasons to travel to Sunderland, but duty had to suffice on this occasion. It's an unremarkable place, until you get to the river - the obvious lifeblood of the town. I still find it strange people are so defined by the places they grow up. Those places in turn are simply defined by how they manage to sustain the people that live there.

Upon entering now, it is impossible to determine if the people have shaped the place, or the place has moulded its residents.

Sadly, I cared little for either.

London has districts just like this entire town. Ships, boatyards and sailors as far as the eye can see. I have always avoided these parts of the great city. There is a transience about it all; a feeling that most of the inhabitants are simply passing through. The 'real' residents of London exist in those places to wring as much money out of the jobbing tourists while they can... like any real Londoner would. Here, however, there is a permanence in the temporary nature of the trade. Even without the docks London would still unmistakably be London. There are many other defining facets to the city. Here, in the north east of the country, it feels as though a loss of this particular trade would completely rob the town of its purpose and identity. I picked up on a constant and much ignored insecurity to the people and place. It made my skin crawl a little, which is no mean feat, but it reminded me of a similar feeling I had walking among the dead. The deceased are rarely aware of their fate. It makes them no less dead, but there is always a creeping edge of knowing that something is a little 'off'.

I had been accompanied on my trip by a special constable. His name was Jenkins, and he knew nothing about the particulars of my trade. I hoped it would stay that way. He did possess an admirable respect for higher authority, which made him very easy to work with. He didn't know me, and was my senior in years and seemingly experience, but after witnessing the deference his immediate superiors gave me at our briefing he fell into line without question. It is a rare trait; I find most people are blinded by the idea that age casts a natural pecking order.

I had very little time or patience for these sorts of petty politics. Every workplace has them, especially civilian vocations with a clear chain of command. There is infighting and backbiting, perceived slights and petty jealousies. I supposed it was an advantage that my own organisation was still very small, and that I was unquestionably in charge of it (partly because only I could do it, but mostly because nobody else wanted to). Even so, all things have their disadvantages; for example, not having any other suitable colleagues to send off to Sunderland for a simple investigation that would more than likely be nothing.

I sent Jenkins off with the luggage to sort out some accommodation. I hoped we wouldn't be staying long, but the journey had been dull and arduous. Jenkins was a fine enough fellow but there was very little overlap in our conversational oeuvres. Most of the trip had been spent in silence. I didn't mind in the least, but I could tell my companion had found it rather uncomfortable. Most genial acquaintances are whiled away with chit-chat about working life. There was very little I could tell of my own recent dealings, certainly nothing that would have been considered polite conversation: exorcisms, hunting an Eachy in the sewers below Kensington, and investigating a group of performing illusionists (turned out one of them was cheating and using real magic).

I wandered along the quay, filling my pipe. The air had a tang of salt and the stench of industry, with a shade of something altogether more unwholesome. There was a lively hustle and bustle. Boats bobbed up and down at their moorings as goods were unloaded and then re-packed. Beyond the first line of boats closest to shore there were a few rows further out. Then I spotted the reason I had been called; a ship anchored a half-mile offshore - alone and in quarantine.

I inhaled deeply. Smoking always helped me to think. I believe it's the simple ritual and habit of it. My centring activity, something so mundane and utterly human in nature that never fails in bringing me back to myself and clearing my mind. In this case it also helped to mask the acrid vapour of tar and vinegar that was being burned in a brazier that I had passed. An effort to cleanse the 'bad air' that had been held under suspicion of spreading the aliment.

There was very little movement on the ship that I could see from my vantage point. It looked stark, certainly out of place. If I had not known the situation beforehand, a simple observation would have raised a question in my mind about its position. The tableau intensified the feeling of unease I had already picked up in the town. Most fittingly it was like an illness had set in, and the symptoms were just beginning to show themselves. Which, of course, was precisely the case and my reason for being there.

A man promptly vomited over the edge of the quay into the water. I snapped out of my reverie and reminded myself to keep a small distance from the populace, at least until I knew the precise nature of the epidemic that had begun to take hold of the town.

It was thought to have originated in Bengal, India. It quickly spread across Asia, killing hundreds of thousands of people, travelled slowly through Russia, into Europe and down to Africa. It showed no signs of stopping; there were no medical solutions.

The quarantined ship came from the Baltics. The government had been very clear that any ships from that region were to be stopped from docking and held in quarantine to be fully checked. It would seem the desperation of the industry to keep rolling along had outweighed caution.

A few unwell sailors went into the port town and did what sailors inevitably do… thus the disease had a toehold. People started to get ill, and began to die.

Governments barely bat an eyelid when a few people die, but it's only when an awful lot of people die they begin to take a serious interest. It's reactionary, perhaps even callous, but there are a lot of people to govern in the British Empire; it would seem a system of dealing with things as they crop up is preferred to making sure such things never come to pass. I only observe all of this because I had to make my case to Her Majesty Queen Victoria herself as to why such an approach would be ill advised in my particular arena.

Disease, though fatal and difficult to contain, is a much nicer problem to deal with when compared to marauding armies of the damned. It was a short audience and Her Majesty was swift in extending my department's reach and weight.

In this particular case, disease seemed to be an easily identifiable culprit. The outbreak was somewhat expected; its progress had been marked as it slithered across nations in a seemingly inexorable march to our own island.

I read the reports of the outbreak with interest, but a few details rang hollow in my mind when compared to those from the continent (at least, in the very early stages). From what I could piece together, no residents initially died from any contact with the sailors from the ship that had slipped through quarantine. Indeed, there had been illness, but it seemed to be of a milder strain. Once a dozen or so people had fallen into fits of vomiting and cramps, the sailors were bundled back onto their boat and put out to anchor, precisely where the vessel rested upon our arrival.

The sickness abated, the residents recovered. The local papers proclaimed it a near miss, and praised the swift action of the physicians and local constabulary in stamping out a possible epidemic. Unfortunately, the praise was given too hastily. A week after the initial flush of illness subsided, a fresh wave of disease washed over the port and began taking lives. The deaths were indiscriminate and unpleasant in their swift duration.

It was reported time and again that no new ships had broken quarantine, and the original ship had been locked down tight.

There was enough in these events to pique my curiosity, and set my gut trembling at the idea of something intangible at play.

Once Jenkins had returned from securing our billet we set about arranging a boat to take us out to the quarantined ship. I showed official documents and even invoked the Queen's authority, but the locals had rightfully become wary and refused to pilot us. I managed to secure a small skiff, and Jenkins made a manful attempt at rowing us across the estuary to the lonesome vessel. The poor chap seemed to work up quite a sweat. I would have offered to take a turn, but I didn't want to injure his pride.

We clambered aboard the vessel using nets that they had thrown across the top-rail. I'm not of a particularly nautical bent, but even I was aware of the perceived indignity of using the boatswain's chair. Jenkins would have undoubtedly been glad of it, as I heard him huffing rather loudly as he clambered up behind me. I had asked him to keep his jacket on to conceal his pistol, though upon reflection that might have seemed a little unkind. After all, firearms would be no use in our investigation and I had more useful weapons and protections about my person. It's always best to keep these things a mystery to a stranger, as it's much better to be underestimated.

I'm always underestimated.

The crew seemed wary of us once we were on deck. They had been ravaged by their confinement. It was clear supplies to the ship had been sparse, and probably of low quality. It was difficult to imagine that the port would do its best to keep them in comfort during the length of their quarantine after unleashing a sickness. Though, one might hope for common humanitarian decency? We often have to hope for things that are, in fact, rare but which should be commonplace.

The captain approached. He tried to muster some of the dignity of his position, but it was virtually impossible. His eyes were sunken, and the skin of his jowls hung loosely about his chin. His clothes were obviously far too big for his haggard frame. I assumed his belt had once strained about his girth; now the buckle clinked loosely as he stumbled across the planks of his vessel.

"I'm Captain Ryba. I'll not offer my hand, as I wouldn't expect you to take it." His voice had a heavy Slavic lilt, but his intonation was weak and breathy.

I thrust my own hand out toward him. "On the contrary, Captain. I'm very glad to meet you. In fact, I hope my presence might aid you in your current struggles."

Ryba tentatively shook my hand, his grip as shaky as his countenance. "You're a brave man, Mr...?"

"Pope." I paused to look around at the crew that had gathered. "And bravery has very little to do with it, Captain. Apart from malnourishment you all seem to be in decent health. Tell me, have any of your crew fallen to the sickness that made it to the port?"

Captain Ryba looked about as though assessing his ships compliment. "Nay, Mr Pope. I've tried telling the port authorities the same for the past two weeks when they've delivered our scraps."

"It would seem, excepting your poor rations, that you have in fact been rather fortunate," I ventured.

"Really? If this is good fortune, sir, I'd be unsettled to experience your brand of hardship," said Ryba.

I smiled, but I could tell from the captain's face that it looked more like a grimace. "You have avoided the sickness that made it to land. Many people have perished; you all have managed to keep your lives. However, I'm not here to debate your fortune, good or otherwise. I'm here to discover how you brought the sickness to this place."

"I'll stop you there, Mr Pope. There's nothing on this ship that could possibly…"

I raised my hand. "Please, Captain, I'm not making accusations, or trying to place blame. I'm simply seeking the facts behind the current crisis in the hope that I might be able to stop it. I have no concerns over your liability or consequent punishment if you have done anything wrong. It has no bearing or consequence on my aims." I reached into my jacket pocket and handed over my credentials. "You'll see here, I'm acting upon the direct instructions of Her Majesty Queen Victoria. If you help my investigation you may gain an ally that could aid you in turn if any unpleasant accusations are directed towards you once the situation is resolved."

Captain Ryba chuckled. "Lots o' fancy talk for 'I scratch your back, and you might slap mine if I choke.'"

"Then we have an understanding?"

"Aye. I reckon we do." The captain motioned towards one of the gathered seamen behind him. "Jaromir will show you around the ship, and answer any questions you have. He's my first mate. His word is my word."

The man named Jaromir shuffled forward. He was a wretched specimen; unlike the captain, he hadn't begun the quarantine with a plump waist. He had a wiry frame and now looked positively skeletal. The first mate tugged on a lock of hair in deference.

The captain slapped the poor fellow's back, and I thought he would surely crumple into a pile of rags and dust. "You hear me, Jaromir? Tell these men what they want to know. Maybe they send us some proper vittles, eh?" At this, Ryba inclined his head toward me and gave a wink that implied more good humour than was present in our relationship.

"Wh-what w-would you like to see?" asked Jaromir.

"Are you quite all right, sir?" enquired Jenkins. It was a fair question. The first mate had an unfocused look to his eyes, sweat was trickling freely down his forehead, and his speech spoke more of delirium than nervousness.

"I forgot about Jaromir's stutter. Not to worry, he only has it when he breathes, eh Jaromir?" Another booming slap of camaraderie that should have propelled the unfortunate crewman towards the waves. Ryba seemed to re-assess his second in command. "Now I look at you closely, you don't seem all that good." A glimmer of suspicion flared in Ryba's eyes. "You've been at the restricted stores haven't you? Huh?"

Jaromir simply swayed in place as the air was rent with an abominable burst of flatulence. The smell of excrement that followed quickly confirmed the man had passed substantially more than wind. Upon soiling himself, Jaromir's body finally caught up with the state of current affairs and gave up, resulting in him crumpling to the deck.

Ryba sighed. "Danek, Casimir, take the first mate to a secluded bunk. Don't let anyone else near him." The crewmen promptly removed their superior, leaving an ugly smear behind that was quite swiftly dealt with by a very attentive cabin boy.

The captain turned back to us, his charm trying to fill the void of awkwardness. "My apologies, gentlemen. I'll be pleased to assist you personally with your enquiries."

I raised an eyebrow.

Ryba's shoulders slumped. "I know how this looks, eh? But there is a good explanation for it. This isn't the same sickness they have on the land. None of my crew has perished. The only ones that get ill are the ones that are desperate enough to go against my express orders." His face hardened suddenly. I caught a glimpse of a sea captain that would unquestionably face the full ferocity of nature on the open oceans without quailing. "Once these men recover from their illness they will be dealt with appropriately."

"Very well, Captain." I replied. "I'm happy to hear you out. Let us begin with the source of this illness, shall we? It looks awfully similar to what has afflicted the town. It certainly has a comparable stench."

"Aye, that I'll grant you, Mr Pope. When you sail with a full complement for a few weeks, then get held in port for longer, you'd think your nose might become accustomed to a certain level of stench, but this sickness is something else." He turned away and motioned for us to follow. "This way, if you please. If I have answers you're welcome to them. I'll be damned if I can parse it." The remainder of the crew parted for their captain. He barked a few brusque orders on his way to a stairway below decks. The beleaguered souls slowly responded and went about their usual duties. There was the odd sideways glance and sneer as Jenkins and I followed the captain. One can only assume they thought us the cause of their ills, and not a possible solution. I could hardly blame them; their situation was utterly wretched.

Ryba was right about one thing. The smell as we ventured below decks was an assault on our senses. The captain carried a small lamp as we descended to the very bottom of his hold. The stairs creaked and protested, the air became closer, and there was a calmness about it as we stepped below, the water mere inches beyond the knotty planks.

The small circle of light encompassed a lone crewman sitting slumped over on a crate. The captain delivered a sharp jab to his ribs. It had the desired effect. He was as malnourished as the rest of the crew, but this one had a sharpness to his gaze. It certainly hadn't affected his mind as much as the others.

The captain grasped the man's face in a huge claw, and squeezed what little flesh made up his cheeks. "Ony. I'll ask you once. If you lie I'll know, and you'll go into the sea on our way home. Nobody will know or care. I'll tell your family you deserted them. Eh? You hear me?"

"S-s-sir?"

"I asked you to stand guard on these stores, eh? I told you nobody is to touch them. Not a single person should drink from those barrels, eh?" Ryba put his other hand behind his guard's head; it looked as though he might crush his skull with a twitch of his thumbs. "Yet here is old Jaromir, desperate, mad with hunger and thirst. Did he ask you for this water? Did he eat the tainted hardtack?"

Ony didn't hesitate. It seemed the captain's threats were not baseless. "Yes, Cap'n, I gave him some. I'll admit it. The man was near dyin' on 'is feet. Didn't see the harm in rollin' the dice to give him a bit of a chance." It was difficult to hear the words clearly as Ryba hadn't slackened his grip on the man's face.

"Bah!" The captain threw the man against the hull of the boat with a hollow echoing thud. "See what desperation does? You go find Jaromir right now, Ony. He's in sickbay away from the others. You're to look after him. Be the only one close to him. If you catch it too, serves you right, and let it take you." Then Ryba stooped down and looked the crewman in the eye; a stare with the intensity of a raging squall. "If I come to find you profited in this exchange, I'll stick you myself and strap you to the bow as bait. We'll need to catch our own provisions on the way back."

With that Ony scuttled up the stairs, leaving us with a possibly psychotic sailor in a secluded and cramped space. I could tell Jenkins had a similar concern, and I gently placed my hand on his arm. I felt his tension reduce but not dissipate entirely.

Ryba made an attempt to lighten the mood with his misplaced charm. It was fascinating to see his switch from ferocity to amiability, like an actor playing two opposing roles on the same stage. "Good men are hard to find. Can't expect them all to keep their heads in circumstances like this. I suppose you're wondering if I'm good for the threats I was bandying about?"

"No," I replied. "I have no doubt you have it in you, Captain. How you run your affairs is entirely up to you. I will reiterate, so we fully understand one another. I only care for your situation to the extent that it has any bearing on my own."

"Huh. I do believe I've caught fish with warmer blood than yours, Mr Pope. Sounds fair enough to me." Ryba picked up his lamp and lit more that were hanging from the rafters. The oil and wax were low quality and burned with a yellow glow that was quickly absorbed by any surface it touched.

"See anything strange, gentlemen?" asked the captain.

Jenkins shrugged. I could still sense his tension. He was expecting violence; I wondered why he hadn't from the moment we came aboard.

"I assume you mean the malnourished crew with a hold quarter-full of water and ship's biscuit? Yes, that does seem a little at odds, doesn't it?" I replied.

Ryba perched his ample posterior onto a nearby crate. It creaked ominously, but held firm. "I'll be totally honest with you, Mr Pope. We are short one member of the crew that set out from the Baltic Sea." He removed his hat and swept a huge hand through a greasy matt of hair. "Our chief mate."

"The man responsible for your cargo. Seems rather careless to lose a man like that, Captain."

"Aye. Could be you're right. But I'm not completely convinced he was the only one that was lost."

"Come now, Captain, you're confusticating the story. You tell me you've only lost one man, then suspect more are missing. Please lay it out plainly for us," I said.

Ryba gave a great rattling sigh. "You'll think me mad."

I smiled. "You'd be surprised. I have a very high bar for oddity."

"I suspected we had a stowaway. And Vitaly, the chief mate, was helping them - hiding them. At a guess, I'd say the stowaway brought some sort of ill with them." He pointed a meaty thumb towards the barrels behind him. "All of that water is contaminated. Brings on the sickness those crewman that first went ashore had. The sickness my first mate is wrestling with now. It's unpleasant, sure enough, but it don't seem deadly. Not like that which has taken hold of the town. I don't know how this water got tainted, but anything it touches goes the same way. We had a barrel burst over a few crates of the food stores. It all has the same effect." He fixed me with a stare. "Any ideas?"

"A few," I replied. "May I take a closer look?"

"Of course, I would warn caution, but you seem like a careful man."

117

I motioned for Jenkins to follow me with a lamp. As I got a few paces from the barrels, a scent assaulted me. A spasm of disgust must have passed across my features.

"See how desperate my men are? Plain to tell it's unwholesome by the stench, but still they risk it to slake a thirst or feel the weight of some grub in their bellies." To punctuate the point he spat to the side.

Jenkins tried to keep as much distance as possible, but I needed to illuminate the scene. I stooped to look at the floor around the cargo. It was clear to see where the tainted water had been spilled. As it dried it had left a crystalline residue, much like salts left over from evaporated seawater, but this substance had a slight mauve hue. I instructed Jenkins to collect samples. I always liked to take a few curiosities back to the office for our scientists to examine.

I covered my nose and mouth with a handkerchief and pried open a barrel. The smell intensified markedly. As expected, the container was around two thirds full. The only other point of note was a pearlescent slick on the water's surface. Some sort of oil, I guessed. Certainly a substance that should not be in a ship's drinking water.

I closed the barrel once I was sure I would find nothing else to help the enquiry. The stench lessened immediately. The smell had a strange consistency; it was undoubtedly rank in nature, but there were subtitles within that gave me pause.

"Captain, did you keep a store of live fish on board?" I enquired.

Ryba snapped out of a reverie of his own; he'd drifted off a little, while I had busied myself. I guessed that the hunger was gnawing at him being so close to temptation. "Hmmm, oh, no. Anything we caught en route was eaten fresh. We weren't transporting any either. This trip was mostly timber." He gave a wry grin. "It would seem our cargo was not considered hazardous, as that was promptly unloaded before we were sent into our current state of purgatory."

I raised an eyebrow. "I see. I'll be sure to request that it is reclaimed and returned to you. To ensure safety, of course. We can't have anyone profiting from your bad luck before the all-clear is given, can we? I don't suppose you were paid before you were quarantined either?"

"You're a perceptive gentleman, Mr Pope."

"It would seem there is a whiff of corruption on the air, as well as this sickening aroma." I turned back to the captain with purpose. "I've seen all I need to here, Captain Ryba. I want to assure you I'll do my very best to improve your circumstances. I can confidently conclude that you didn't intentionally initiate this series of events. Though you did, unknowingly, carry the source of the sickness to these shores."

"Beg pardon, I'm not sure I take your meaning."

"You did have a stowaway, Captain. Let's go back up to the deck; I'd enjoy a breath of fresh air. I only need one more account from your good self before we depart. I'd like to know a little more about how the chief mate left your employ."

The sun had begun to dip in the sky; an inexorable fall to the horizon behind the buildings of the town. The air was fresh in comparison to below decks; the light seemed bright and harsh. The breeze cooled the sweat on my brow, and I felt refreshed by it. Captain Ryba had followed us. The light showed anew how haggard and wretched he was. Desperation had permeated his very being. It was clear to me that this was a man with nothing left to lose.

"Do you smoke, Captain?" I asked.

"I did, aye. Haven't had a lungful in a long while."

I handed him a pouch of tobacco. I always kept a few small fripperies in my jacket for a bit of gentle coercion. In this case I was motivated by pity. I resolved to myself that I would rake the harbour master over the coals when I got back to port. "Consider it a small gift, as you've been so helpful," I said.

"That's very kind of you, Mr Pope. Greatly appreciated." He shuffled his feet a little, and leaned towards me conspiratorially. "It'll go a very short way to helping those I'm responsible for though. I wonder if I might impress upon you the desperation of our situation. I'm a proud man, but begging for our lives is not beneath me. Another week and I fear we will begin to perish."

I placed a hand on the captain's shoulder. I was surprised to find that the man's overcoat was performing a grand illusion; the body beneath the fabric with far less substantial than I had reckoned. "I promise to do everything in my power, Captain Ryba."

He straightened up, seemingly satisfied, and gave a grin. "I reckon that power might be quite considerable if I'm a judge of anything. You'll have my eternal gratitude."

"I'm not in need of your gratitude, sir. I need just one more story from you, then we can get back and begin straightening the strands of this tangled mess."

Ryba found a perch, out of need rather than comfort, I assumed. "Vitaly. I'll admit my own failings. I didn't keep a close eye on him this voyage. He was a dependable man; I didn't have many worries on him doing what he was supposed to. Sort of man you trust with the stores, you see. Some will hoard or try to profit. Vitaly kept it all pretty straight. I knew the side-games he had going on; he would make a point of hinting at them to me, as a roundabout way of asking permission. He'd sailed with me for years so I gave him a bit of leeway. Better the devil you know, sometimes.

"I got reports a few days out from making land that the stores were running short. It don't take long for the grumbles on deck to reach my ears. A captain needs to be sensitive to these things. Moaning can turn quickly to mutiny. I may be in charge, but the crew ain't dumb enough not to realise they have the numbers. Here was the strange part; Vitaly looked me square in the eye, and lied to me. Told me he'd made a mistake. That he hadn't taken enough on board before we set sail. I don't know what he was covering up, and I didn't get the chance to find out. I had plenty on my mind to get us into port, and then we were quarantined.

"Again, I feel as though I failed. I heard reports that Vitaly was agitated by the news. A disproportionate reaction, I recall thinking. As I said, we'd been sailing together for years, we've been quarantined plenty o' times. I was doing my best to negotiate supplies with the harbour master." The captain sighed. He looked utterly exhausted. "The first night we were moored out here there was a shout of 'man overboard'. It had been a condition of supply that I policed my own men to keep the quarantine. I ran to the rail and was told there had been two separate splashes. We set light to some pitch and chucked it into the water, but nothing broke the surface. No splashing, no movement at all.

"Vitaly was a strong swimmer, but not even he could have got away without us hearing him." Ryba pointed a finger at me. His eyes shone briefly, and the intensity of the man in his prime flared back up for a moment. "There's only one thing that keeps hanging in my mind. Two splashes. I can't help thinking a stowaway got my old friend killed."

Jenkins did a manful job of getting us back to the harbour. He seemed relieved to get off the ship, and glad that we didn't encounter any violence. It made me wonder how experienced he was with the physical side of law enforcement. It didn't seem to daunt him, but the concept obviously wasn't welcome. A nice idea, but any reticence on that front while accompanying me could be disastrous.

The next part of the investigation had to be undertaken in darkness, so I whiled away the late afternoon by engaging the harbour master in conversation regarding the treatment of Captain Ryba and his crew. I've found silence to be a powerful negotiation tactic. I made a polite and robust case to the man in charge, then stood impassively in front of him while he railed against my assertions. Once he had run out of words, I continued to look upon him with an air of icy indifference. It creates an instantly uncomfortable atmosphere. The kind of situation most people cannot deal with properly. There seems to be a human instinct to fill any void that is encountered. By the time the harbour master was stuttering and spluttering I turned on my heel and left.

I dined with Jenkins at our lodging house and made a few attempts at idle conversation. I discovered my associate was a family man, responsible for two young girls. I was somewhat taken aback as he didn't strike me as the attentive father he obviously was. Every time he spoke about his girls his face was bathed in a fervent glow.

I still find pleasure in being surprised, even mildly so. I am used to my initial assumptions and observations of people and situations being accurate.

At dusk we struck out from the lodgings. I was gratified to spy a mid-sized boat being loaded with provisions under the supervision of the harbour master. This time I was confident in my assumption that it was headed to aid Captain Ryba and his crew. I tipped my hat towards the busy bureaucrat in charge, and he hurriedly returned my gesture with many a grand and obsequious flourish.

We had a bit of a tromp ahead of us. The estuary of most rivers tended to be a little busy for what needed to be done next. Jenkins held a lamp out in front. We followed the course of the River Wear away from the docks, through the town and past the buildings, as the main settlement faded into the encroaching darkness of the night.

The dark has never held any fear for me. It has always been a great comfort. Better for concealment, easier to make a swift get-away. Though I could tell Jenkins felt differently. His breathing became ragged, his gait more laboured. He made the arc of the lamp wider in an effort to see more of the ground ahead of him.

My efforts to ease his worries fell flat. Empathy is not one of my stronger traits. I did tell him that I'd be sure to let him know as and when things began to get dangerous, which I was quite certain they would in due course.

I alluded to the power of silence earlier. You may wonder how I came to learn such a lesson. There is truly no such thing as absolute silence in the natural world; even when you believe you are experiencing silence, it is in fact extreme quiet. There are always noises... a low hiss of a gas lamp, the rustle of a breeze in the trees, your own breath entering and exiting your lungs, the blood pumping through your head.

Absolute silence is a supernatural occurrence. It envelops everything, and you feel as though you are standing in a vacuum.

True to my word, I let Jenkins know that the danger had begun as soon as I realised we'd entered such a bubble of muted existence. By the look of him, he'd already come to the same conclusion himself. He was pale, and had a sheen of greasy sweat on his brow despite the cold stiff breeze we were walking against.

We were following a very rough and rarely used path that followed the course of the river on the northern bank. The grass and bushes had begun to overtake the way forward, and it was getting more difficult to make progress. I was sure we wouldn't need to go further, as it began to feel as though the natural terrain was forcing us in a distinct direction.

All of a sudden, Jenkins swung his lamp in a wide arc out towards the water. He gave a cry, its volume hideously loud in the eerie silence. "Look, sir! A young girl, floating in the river. She'll surely drown."

Before I could grab him, he'd jumped from the bank and was in the water up to his thighs, wading towards something I knew was assuredly not a young girl in danger.

I dived after Jenkins, realising the trap he'd fallen into. He was reaching a hand out to what he believed to be a young girl. Suddenly, a figure broke the surface of the river, and an acrid stench filled the air. The silence deepened, becoming a sonic pressure in my head. I jumped onto Jenkins' back and tried to snatch his arm away from the creature that had appeared.

Too late!

Jenkins yelled in pain. I surged forward, and pressed my hand onto the head of the creature that had clamped itself onto my companion. A second shriek rented the silence, every utterance a painful percussive force.

Jenkins fell back, and the creature reeled away from my grasp. It was steeling itself to attack me, snatching a look in my direction before it did so. I held my palm out, displaying what had inflicted the pain upon it.

"Evening, Nelly. I was hoping for a quiet chat," I panted, trying to keep my voice level.

The creature stopped, slowly rose to its full height, and became wary. "Pope, is it?" It raised an unnaturally long arm with spindly fingers towards me. "Not a nice ice-breaker that, is it?"

I gently shook the iron amulet in my hand towards her. "Just a precaution, Nelly, or should I say Peg? Jenny, perhaps? I had to protect my man here. He nearly took your bait."

The creature's fingers got within a few inches of my hand before suddenly pulling away as it felt the prickle of the iron near its skin. "Gah! Nasty stuff. If you wanted to talk, Pope, you could simply ask. Bring an offering and I'm quite accommodating.

"You can call me what you like. All them names are the ones your folk give us, not what we're rightly called. Downright insulting, if you ask me. 'Peg Prowler, Nelly Longarms, Jenny Greenteeth. My teeth look green to you?" She treated me to a wide grimace of needle sharp teeth. In the limited light they glistened with a sickly tinge of red.

I shot a look over to Jenkins. He had reached the river bank and was laying down, his feet dangling in the water. He was breathing heavily and sobbing quietly, cradling the hand he'd reached out. "Let me see, Jenkins," I asked, keeping a close watch on the hag. His right hand was missing both the little and ring fingers. "Take your tie off and bind it tightly around your wrist. Get right out of the water. I'll get you back to town as soon as I can." I heard him shift his body as I turned my attention back to the creature.

"What you got for me, Pope? I may as well bugger off if there's nothing in this little meeting for me," said the hag. She was now quite relaxed, bobbing in the river's current. I knew we were very much in her preferred surroundings, though she was being careful to stay out of my reach.

"I'd say you took a decent snack from my man there, Groac'h," I ventured.

"So you do know our rightful name. All the more insulting you stared with the nicknames then, really. We'll call that little morsel an introduction. I'll be wanting more for what you're after. It's a particularly interesting tale an' all."

"How about you make do with the taste of blood you've had, tell me what you know, and I'll decide if it deserves a reward? Something tells me you might profit from me looking into what's going on here as much as I will." I paused. "Can I put this iron away? I'd much rather talk without threats, but do know I have a few packets of iron filings in my jacket pocket. If you try anything, I will taint your water."

The atmosphere lightened. I heard the breeze singing in the trees on the bank. I took that as my answer, and lowered my hand.

"Funny way of talking without threats, by making an even bigger one. Strange folk, you mortals. This is like a cow coming up to you and striking a bargain for its milk. Your man was fair game. He wasn't savvy enough, and paid a light price for it," said the hag.

"Any game is easy with the right bait. Showing the father of two daughters a young girl in danger isn't really playing fair."

"Hmmm, if you say so. What did you see, Pope? He saw a girl like his daughters in danger. What fear of yours did I pluck at?"

"Just you, Groac'h, just you."

"Interesting. Either means you have no fear, or there's nothing you hold dear."

"Do you have a story to tell?"

"Tell you what, you tell me what you really saw and I'll share everything that these old eyes have spied over the last few weeks. How's that sound?"

I took a look around towards Jenkins. He was suitably preoccupied with not bleeding to death. I edged as close to the hag as I dared, and hissed my reply. "I saw a boy looking lost and frightened. He reminded me greatly of myself at around the age of thirteen. Is that ample payment?"

The Groac'h stopped mid-stream and emerged a little from the water. Her gaze intensified, a renewed interest had been kindled in her. "I reckon so. I daresay there's an interestin' story behind what you saw, Mr Pope. I wonder if anyone is likely to hear it? Knowledge is as good as currency in our line, and I'd say you've given me plenty."

"It's settled then. Out with it, if you please? The river is beginning to get a little chilly."

"Ha! Like a warm spring, this stretch. Though I suppose you are warm blooded, ain't you? I'll try not to keep you, but it's a tale of decent length. Lots happenin' in the River Wear lately. Going to be forced north up to the Tyne if I'm any judge. This river has been spoiled. No fresh meat coming my way if I stay.

"I smelled its arrival on the incoming tide. Unmistakable stench, it was. Trouble, them lot always are. I went up to the estuary to see if it was coming my way, or heading north. It was the strangest thing. The stink was staying out to sea, like it couldn't make it the last little way.

"Turned out it was just a delay. One night there was a bit of commotion on a ship moored out deep. A few shouts and some splashing, and that smell entered the water. It was like a flash of light shooting through the whole river. That's power, that is. Raw and ready to take on whatever is silly enough to stand in its way. Needless to say, I ain't that addled just yet. I stayed in the shadows and watched it all play out."

Once I'd got the hag talking I knew better than to disturb her. Any reason to deviate or embellish would run the risk of her account altering, and it would extend my stay in the freezing river. By this point I couldn't feel my feet. I still had the iron close to hand, but I was fairly certain this encounter would not turn sour. We each knew enough about the other to know any aggravation would result in mutual destruction. Being prepared to die is a surprisingly strong form of protection. Very few other beings are willing to give their lives for a cause.

So far what she had to say had confirmed my suspicions from visiting the quarantined ship. Something that lived in water had been stored in the barrels. They sullied one barrel at a time as the voyage wore on. I could only guess how it had snared the sailor into helping it, but all creatures have their wiles. He paid for his weakness in the end.

"The sailor was dead before they surfaced in the river. She'd pulled him under as soon as they were in the water; drained him quick as you'd like, but kept the body to feast on. She looked a starved thing - I wasn't shocked to see her rip the man apart in a frenzy. Really wasn't much left of him once she was done. Seemed to restore her some, any road. Naiads can be ruthless when they're on the offensive."

I was intrigued. The possible waterborne creatures that could taint an entire river are a small pool, if you'll excuse the pun. But I was still surprised that a Naiad, the spirit of a waterway, had ventured to Britain to challenge the local powers.

"Now, if a stench and a flash of power is notable to old Groac'h here, you bet the residing river spirit is going to have noticed too. Ol' Naiad Wear was up here as quick she could swim to see what might be threatenin' her waters. Surprised she weren't here before me, truth be told. Naiads are extra sensitive to their own kind. She must have been way downstream when she felt the change.

"So, the Spirit o' the Wear turns up to tell the newcomer to bugger orf. As you do. Seems like this new one is all haughty. Reckons she's of some ancient line of Naiads from the Rhine. Anyway, seems she weren't bluffin'. Even in her reduced state she took on Wear and killed her outright. Savage, it was. Almost enough to turn my stomach, and that's sayin' something.

"So there it is. The river's been polluted with Naiad blood. Tainted. Nothing good will come from the water. Nothing will grow, and only disease will be spread until a new spirit asserts itself."

That was all I needed. I'd suspected a lot of what I'd heard, but a few points had mildly surprised me. "A new spirit? Surely the newcomer took up residence? Why hasn't she begun to cleanse the waters?"

"Ha! Not a bit of it. She muddied the flow and flounced off. She'll be after bigger prizes than this. As I said, a drop of self-importance about that one. We'll have a bit of a wait until a new spirit can establish power."

I frowned. "How long can that take?" I didn't know for sure how a river spirit manifested.

The hag stood up to her full height, and pointed upstream. For the first time I noted a dull glimmer of light coming from the riverbed under overhanging foliage. "I dunno really. No idea how long it takes Naiad eggs to hatch, much less grow up enough to put right the damage."

I got Jenkins back to our lodgings and called for a doctor. He'd be a few fingers short, but he'd hold onto his life.

I left at once to strike out in pursuit of the Naiad invader. I received some strange looks when I demanded that any water used in Jenkins' treatment needed to be from the sea, and boiled. I didn't dare let the locals know the source of their ills. I had to report to my seniors so we might begin making a plan.

There would be more disease. More death.

I had a river spirit to hunt.

ᘔᖇᖇᖇᖇ ᖇᖇᖇ

Mr Hopkins pointed out I was writing more about others than myself. I dare say I should have focused a bit more. My mind is wandering towards subjects that will upset me.

Where was I? My learning, that's right. I schooled myself. Had help where I could get it. I worked for anyone that could pay a few coppers. A young lad that had his letters and a legible hand was of use to a lot of folk on our street. I helped with the running of the house and bought more books with my earnings. Didn't matter to me what the books were about, to start with. Any new information was up for grabs. Over time I began to pick and choose more. My interest in the wider world grew as I visited the corners of the growing empire in the dispatches that would come back with the trading ships. I often thought about securing a berth and being on my way, but I had good reasons to stay; two reasons that were getting older and in need of more help.

It's safe to say my life changed the first time I saw a spirit. When I was ten I used to visit an elderly gent, Mr Walton. He enjoyed his books too, but his eyes had begun to betray him. I went along a few times a week to read aloud to him for a few hours in the evening. He was very generous even though I would have done it for nothing, as he always let me borrow from his own collection of books. "No good to me now, young'en," he'd say. "Books need to be read, they ain't made to sit on shelves and rot. They begin to fidget."

One evening in winter, I remember it very well, the chill had begun to turn and I wondered if it was the first signs of spring. I was reading a particularly good collection of Greek myths. The old timer loved legends. He advised me to take note. "Even the most fanciful work of fiction contains a truth," he'd say. After what happened I wondered why he never spoke more plainly. I guess it was some sort of test.

He passed away quite peacefully as I recited Theocritus. I was aware of the very moment it happened. The light and temperature of the room were unchanged, but the atmosphere shifted. It became thick, as though the air itself had set like jelly. I wasn't sure if I could move, but I felt no inclination to. I have never been able to tell if the moment was frozen, or I was frozen while the world continued.

I wasn't alarmed by any of this. It felt quite natural. I was curious. It was new, and I had lived my life in a constant chase for discovery.

The old man sat up in his bed, while at the same time leaving his body behind where it lay. He turned his head and smiled at me, and then pointed towards his desk. For a moment a draw in the bureau glowed. Then he faded, the air melted, and the sensation passed.

Describing death is an odd challenge. How do you describe an absence? For that is what death is.

Death.

I cannot--

ℛℰℱℒℰℭℐℴℕ

It was my first time in Egypt. I can't say I'm in a hurry to return. I didn't mind the arid heat; I have spent some time in the tropics. No, it was the stench. Any large city sitting upon a river with a high ambient temperature cannot escape the smell that those factors combine to create. I felt as though I wore a disapproving grimace at all times, regardless of how I might actually be feeling.

I told my loyal butler of this predicament. He had been good enough to accompany me on this relatively light duty. It was his assurance that the scowl would lend me an imperious air that quite suited my station and situation.

I had a lot on my mind. I was uncomfortable with the task that I had accepted. I have seen war, played my part on a battlefield. It has a simplicity about it - I might even call it an honesty. The enemy is clearly designated, their intentions explicit. The environment I was about to enter was a mire of crossed purposes and hidden agendas.

It was all to do with fragile alliances; Egypt siding with the French, while Britain decided to back the Ottomans. It all caused a little diplomatic unpleasantness. In such cases, where it seems nobody can possibly say anything in public for fear of losing face or causing offence, a lavish and garish function must be organised. I've never really understood this mechanism of statesmanship, but it happens a lot. I wonder if the drink flows and loosens tongues, or if everyone being in the same room reminds us that we have more in common than that which divides us? It is most likely the former.

We had passed through streets of impoverished squalor to draw up to a grand palace with manicured gardens and, absurdly, a lawn. I couldn't help but wonder how many citizens died of thirst for the sake of that grass? This was a moment that my scowl of disapproval actually deepened; I feared it might stick for a time to come.

The smell on the air could not be bought though. We climbed from the carriage onto perfectly levelled gravel. All of the senses were filled with the opulence of the place; all of them except smell. The nose never lies. This party reeked, and I feared it had little to do with the city and its river. I smelled corruption.

My companion uttered a few words of assurance. I knew he was more comfortable in these situations than myself. He soon remembered his position, realising that his behaviour might be seen as inappropriate. We've been through a lot over the years that has helped to bridge the professional distance between us, but I would never claim to have become overly familiar with him. Though this has never precluded a growing mutual fondness.

There was a small greeting party on the large set of steps leading up to the building entrance. It seemed a climb that would test most of the wealthy, well furnished guests that I expected to attend the gathering. Perhaps some of them might lower themselves by using the tradesperson's entrance? We walked past a particularly rotund ambassador who had made camp around two thirds of the way up the steps. A waiter was descending with a glass of champagne and a platter of food. I couldn't help but wonder if shame evaporated in line with vast wealth and privilege?

I nodded to the seated dignitary who returned my greeting while shovelling pastries down his gullet via his flushed and sweaty face. I spied another server exiting the building with a bottle en route to the stranded gentleman, and quietly despaired.

The air was a little cooler inside. We had no jackets to leave in the lobby, but we were politely asked to pass over any weapons we might be carrying, for safekeeping. I flicked my arm and handed over a small pistol that had been concealed up my sleeve. It was all for show, of course. If you don't give them something they assume you're holding back. Better to reveal a little, and mask the reality. It makes everyone feel better, like all involved did their jobs properly, even if they know the larger untruths at play.

Music drifted from the main ballroom as doors opened and closed, giving it a staccato rhythm. It sounded like a waltz. I couldn't recall the last time I had danced; there was a time in my life when it had been a joy to me, but it is remote now - a corner of myself that is cut off, as though it belongs to another person.

Dancing is something that someone does if they have the freedom to do so. It is an act of expression, of joy. For the longest time my life has been one of service; putting the needs of others before my own has been a part of me for so long that I can barely consider an alternative.

With such thoughts bouncing around my mind I entered the grand ballroom through the door being held by my attendant. It felt very strange. A voice to the side announced in accented but perfect English, "Mr Silas Pope, advisor to

Her Majesty Queen Victoria of the United Kingdom of Great Britain and Ireland.''

Eyes swivelled in my direction, but heads didn't turn. Most people would not have noticed it, but I am a man who relies upon details.

Couples danced and twirled around the floor. At the edges of the room small groups formed for discussion and, one assumed, gossip and intrigue. Servants, almost invisible, meandered through the crowds making sure drinks did not go dry, and plates were cleared without the suggestion of a thank you; not a shadow of acknowledgement. This irked me.

Suddenly a hand grabbed my arm and steered me away from the main crowd of partygoers. As I turned, or rather was turned by my companion, my eye caught the gaze of a very attractive young lady. I saw recognition, maybe not of my identity, but certainly of information that I wished to be kept secret. My stomach lurched and I felt a snap of fear.

Our ruse felt completely transparent.

My attendant leaned close to me. "You have been recognised, or rather someone I did not expect to be here who knows my face now knows you are not who you are claiming to be," he hissed.

My breath faltered and became ragged, the fear twisting in my gut as I realised the danger in which I had placed myself.

"Not to worry Jarvis, all is not lost. I have no reason to believe we will be betrayed, not unless the young lady can profit from it," whispered Mr Pope as he pretended to fuss over my necktie and collar. "One small suggestion, if you don't mind. To pass well as me you really should be far more rude to people." He winked and we made our way back into the throng.

- - - - - - -

When I asked Jarvis to pose as my decoy I knew there was the possibility that I'd be placing him in harms way. He accepted it, but I had underestimated the risk considerably. As soon as she spotted that the man announced to the gathering was not, in fact, me I knew it was likely I'd have to sit the poor fellow down with a Sentiment Stone to remove the sting from the experience. Whenever my path crosses hers it is very rare for the outcome to be profitable, at least financially, though it is never without its pleasures.

Adrienne Durrant; I am one of very few people on the face of this Earth who knows that name, and more specifically that it is attached to the lady whose eyes barely brushed across us but clearly took in the significance of what they saw. I spotted her as I held the door open, her back to us but her head tilted ever so slightly around, almost as if she was listening, though not in any way that a general observer would notice. Her hair was pulled tightly up into a braided bun exposing the curve of her neck. Her posture was always poised and alert, but spoke of a lithe fluidity when needed. She was, of course, dressed impeccably. Not in a high, showy fashion but in an understated refined way, so that anyone that knew their business would be able to tell she was actually the most extravagantly dressed lady in the room.

I'll admit I was thrown for a moment. I had not expected her to be here. It is rare my sources are wrong, but it seems an inevitability that Madame Durrant will always have the advantage over me. She is the best of her particular trade, and her life depends upon being one step ahead of everyone she deals with.

Madame Durrant is a professional double agent; a free market spy. Secrets for cash, no morals, no masters, no problem.

I have used her services freely over the course of my career, probably as many times as I have been burned by her when she has served my enemies. It takes a very special kind of person to play the ends against the middle as a career and last half as long as she has. There is no secret to her success; her currency is secrets themselves. She has enough information to get every major player in Europe killed on a whim. Every single one, except me.

I tried my best to direct the disguised Jarvis away from Madame Durrant, even though I knew it was hopeless. She turned to go towards a gaggle of very drunk dignitaries, her eyes scanning us and filing away the details. She is very good. She ignored us completely while signalling to me with the tilt of her shoulder and the flick of her chin that my game had been noticed and that I was in her pocket.

I made a fuss of re-arranging Jarvis' collar while trying to calm him down. He'd noticed the lady and divined the same message, even if he hadn't realised its magnitude. I then offered a little constructive criticism on how he might bolster his performance.

He took my notes to heart by batting away my attentions, scowling down at me and loudly instructing me to 'stop with my infernal fussing!'. I did pause to wonder if he had a little unresolved resentment towards me, or if he was doing an excellent job of masking his concerns with confidence and bluster. He turned sharply on his heel and headed into the party proper.

I took my cue, furrowed my brow, stooped my back a little, and added a barely perceptible hitch in my gait. I was careful to walk a step behind my 'master' with my eyes lowered to make sure they did not connect with any of my 'betters'.

I have always had a passion for the subterfuge of disguise. In particular, when there is no magic involved. Changing the way one looks and acts to inhabit a different persona, to disappear in plain sight. I suppose it is the closest thing to magic without actually being a practitioner. I'm surprised more people don't give it a go as a hobby.

Even though my gaze was lowered my vision did not suffer. I was perfectly aware of my surroundings and the people in the crowds we passed. I was looking for one person in particular, though he was usually very easy to spot. For a master Thaumagere, like myself, he enjoyed the spotlight a little too much. I suppose that might be the Gallic flair for showmanship, but I have never trusted a spy that was comfortable with accolades and fame. I feel it paints a target on one's back. Perhaps if the target is large enough it might not seem worth the bother of aiming precisely?

It is fair to say our minds are wired differently, and that is reflected in the way we conduct our affairs. I speak, of course, about 'L'Effroi', or Victor Souriant as his mother might know him.

I have met the man many times, but as far as I'm aware, I don't believe he knows this. He is the poster boy of French Intelligence. Of course, they don't reveal the true depth or nature of his work; he is hailed as a charismatic diplomat and statesman, but it is an open secret in societal circles that he deals in illicit information. Most nations cannot figure out how he manages to be so successful, but the idiom of 'it takes one to know one' provided me with my answer to this quirky puzzle.

The last time I met Monsieur Souriant I was posing as a Prussian undersecretary. I felt him gently probe the surface of my mind as we made idle conversation. I offered up the misinformation I planned to let slip, while protecting my true thoughts. He was a practitioner, and a relatively skilled one. I continued my research and discovered just how talented he was. As well as finding out how ruthless the man could be.

Below the bonhomie and sparkling good humour there was a heart of ice and a will of iron. I could never manage to gather conclusive evidence, but I have suggestive hints that Souriant has been responsible for acts of torture and mass-murder. I can never pretend that my own hands are clean, but in all of my research I have never uncovered any reasoning behind the man's suspected atrocities. My only moral comfort for the actions I must occasionally undertake is that they are productive; dirty shortcuts to high and pure goals.

The witness statements I took described a petulant man acting out of anger and punishing victims on a whim. They are the ones that dubbed him L'Effroi; 'the Terror' or 'the Dread'. I often wonder if he knows he has that reputation; I would guess that he does, and I would also venture that he rather enjoys it.

I heard him before I saw him. He has an unctuous braying laugh, usually in reaction to a witticism or comment of his own.

I coughed politely - a pre-arranged signal. Jarvis made an excuse to cut off the conversation he was having with an attaché from the Ottoman delegation, and headed towards the washrooms. Large homes and palaces are excellent places to find small hidden corners and secret nooks. It is almost impossible to walk through one of these functions without noticing the whispered conversations and barely audible threats from behind pillars or plush curtains. We made use of one such hiding place.

Jarvis sagged in relief. An excuse to drop his mask, which I had to admit had held up admirably, though I could never tell him so in such effusive tones. "Did you see the man up on the main balcony? Loud laugh, almost oafish demeanour?" I queried.

"Of course," replied Jarvis. "Horrible racket. The French are usually somewhat more refined."

"It's a public persona, don't read too much into it. That is the man you must try to avoid, if at all possible. It is not a disaster if you were to converse, in fact it might actually be helpful in the future if he were to believe that you are me, but it would put you in more danger than I would like." Jarvis seemed a little taken aback by my comment, humbled by my concern. "How good are you at shielding your mind?"

"I have been practising, sir, as per your suggestion."

"Well, that man is possibly the finest mind skimmer in the world. If he were to meet you for any length of time you would risk discovery, and as such mortal peril. Would you like to avoid that test?" I asked.

"Yes, sir. I do believe I would." Jarvis quavered a little. I never questioned the man's bravery or commitment, but I worried that sometimes his sense of duty put him in waters that might be deeper than his talents could stand up in. Something occurred to him. "What of the lady?"

There was only one lady in a room full of women. It was quite obvious to whom Jarvis was referring. "She is a wildcard - it is just as likely that she will help or hinder us. Think of her as the flip of a coin.

"Try to stick with the Ottoman delegates. The French have very little business with them currently, they sided with the Egyptians."

I watched as Jarvis arranged his features back into his facsimile of my character. It was a little unnerving. He really did capture my haughtiness, though I like to think he missed how I playfully undercut it with the suggestion of good humour. "Keep it to small talk. They love complaining about the French, do you think you can manage that for ten minutes?" I asked.

Jarvis arched an eyebrow imperiously. "Only ten minutes? Surely we could speak of nothing else for days?"

I held him briefly by the upper arms in what I thought was an encouraging manner. "Excellent. Good luck, I'll be as quick as I can." With that, Jarvis slipped out of the shadows to return to the party.

I took a few moments to drop my own disguise. If I was to be found wandering around a large private residence, it was best that I was discovered as Silas Pope, rather than an attendant. It is much easier to brush off doing something wrong when you have the social position of someone who believes the normal rules never apply to them. Even if I don't hold with that attitude, I'm never below using it to my advantage.

I left the hiding place as myself once again. I had conducted my research well. I knew precisely where I wanted to go and what I should find when I got there. Sadly, plans are fickle beasts.

I never like to use my powers unless I absolutely must. To use them for frippery is indulgent and unprofessional. I fear it becoming a crutch, that overuse will dull my other more usual skills. It is my last resort, and quite the trump card in a tight spot. With this in mind I threaded my way up the back stairs and into the residential wing of the palace.

There were plenty of people around; some security, some other guests looking for more private spaces for their own entertainment. There was plenty of staff milling about too. All in all it seemed far too overpopulated for what was supposed to be a secure area. To my mind it was suspicious, as it clashed with the intelligence I'd been given.

Moving unseen was simple, sometimes moving in plain sight with a stooped shoulder, shuffling walk and a glazed expression, other times travelling with enough pomp and self-importance that nobody would dare to challenge my presence. It was also simplicity to find places to pause and physically hide as others passed in ignorance. Big houses like this are littered with shadows, curtains and garish artwork; the sort of place one would never dare to play hide and seek with a child for fear of losing them forever.

My feet didn't need the deep, lush carpets to move silently along the hallways. After a few turns the corridors became slightly narrower, the decor more utilitarian. It felt less show, more business. I could imagine the bustle of office work along these halls; secretaries shuttling from door to door, and orders being shouted from behind desks out of view. There is a strange atmosphere or uneasy quiet when you visit a place that usually exists in a bustle and a hurry - like being in a schoolroom out of class hours, or a factory when the machinery is still.

I paused by the door I had been informed contained my quarry. I didn't bother to look about myself; my other senses were cast wide in all directions, and I knew that I would not be disturbed in the time it would take me to pick the lock.

I checked the handle first, it is surprising how many trainees forget this simple step.

Lock picking is a wonderful pastime for anyone without nefarious intent. It trains a deftness of hand and mind. You push back everything in your head and focus on the simple feel of the tools in your fingers, sensing and judging how you are moving the invisible mechanism. It is the closest I ever get to feeling like I'm using magic when I am, in fact, not.

My enjoyment was spoiled when I received a massive surge of power, which I had to quickly displace by blowing a hole through the wall on the opposite side of the corridor.

I had been foolish.

It was a magical booby-trap. I should have sensed it, or at the very least precautioned against it. I chastised myself, quickly opening the lock, slipping into the room, and replacing the trap that I had triggered - or as close an approximation as I could muster. There was no doubt that the magical detonation would have drawn attention. Anyone in the know would guess their trap had been tripped. I hoped if they inspected the door to see an enchantment in place they might assume a misfire of some sort. If it were me, I would still check the room I had protected.

I didn't have time to do what I had originally planned.

The room was much larger than I had imagined; it actually had three doors entering it from the hallway, which seemed strange as they were not present on the other side of the wall. I gave them all a quick look to discover that they were in fact cosmetic. Doors affixed into the walls that did not open at all. It pricked something in my mind, but I ignored it for now.

There was a large table in the middle of the room, with various maps of the region and beyond strewn across it. Lots of papers were scattered around, with ashtrays and empty cups dotted amongst the organised carnage. The room felt like a communal meeting space; far too large to be a personal office. I briefly considered that I had made a mistake, before recalling the trap that should have killed me when I entered. Someone felt there was something worth protecting here.

Under the large table surface were three solid repositories holding it up. They seemed identical as I viewed them, except for the magical field that surrounded the one on the left.

The magic was solid and cloying. It made the air shimmer. There was a heat and a weight to it. As I ventured closer it was difficult to catch my breath. I muttered a few lines of an incantation to myself; I needed to visualise what was in front of me.

It was a mess. A twisted tangle; knot upon knot of power had been spun and fused together. It was a magical safe combination, one that would take hours to unravel and crack. One that I had no hope of overcoming in the time I had. I wasn't completely sure I could master it at my leisure.

I gave up on achieving my goal. I had come for a certain piece of information - one that might improve our nation's lot in the region.

If I couldn't have it, the next best thing was for nobody to have it at all.

I could not pick apart the magic surrounding the repository, and had no doubt there was a sturdy physical safe contained within. But I had a notion that I might use the power surrounding the prize as a conduction medium. The spell was not a barrier, as such, it was a lock.

I strode across the room, picked up the longest poker I could find by the fire (I supposed it could be chilly at night?) and knelt as far away from the cupboard as I could; far enough away not to feel a physical influence from the magic. I hooked the handle on the repository door and opened it. The safe was small and of a common design. Without the magical protection I would have cracked it in minutes.

I pressed the poker up to the safe door, feeling resistance in the air; it was like pushing it through treacle. Once I had metal on metal contact I sent power along the rod. The safe began to heat up.

I was conscious of the time. There had been running feet, hurried conversations, and a messenger had been sent off to find someone of higher seniority. I noticed that the door I had entered through wasn't tested, and assumed the trap was a known danger to the regular security.

By now the metal of the safe around where the poker contacted it was glowing red. I saw curls of smoke peeling from the cracks of the door. As the patch of metal began to turn white, molten ore ran out of the bottom, burning through the repository and the carpet underneath.

I removed the poker, stood it back by the fireplace and considered my escape.

- - - - - - -

Playing Mr Pope is not a chore at all. I spend a lot of time observing him, trying to guess his moods, his needs. Over the years I have become acquainted to most of his habits and curious foibles. There is a marked difference between knowing and being. It is impossible for the greatest of actors to properly immitate Mr Pope, for he keeps so much of himself elsewhere, unreachable.

My pastiche has served us well on a few occasions, but I felt rather undone from the off this time. The young lady had me pegged straight away, which made me nervous.

I re-entered the main gathering with the simple instructions to avoid the young lady and the French spy. I was heading straight for the general safety of the Ottoman delegates when a light hand touched my shoulder. I barely felt it, but its command was inarguable.

"Mr Pope! I thought we had lost you to some dull business or other. I simply must introduce you to someone." Of course, it was the lady. To my horror she was about to introduce me to the only other person in the room who I had been instructed to avoid. "This is Monsieur Souriant. I'm sure you already knew that, of course."

The lady turned her head towards the French spy but her eye lingered on me and her lip curled up into a smile, that under any other circumstances would have been breathtakingly seductive. In this context I felt as though I was a small mammal that had been cornered by an apex predator.

I rallied as best I could. "Of course, Monsieur. A pleasure to finally make your acquaintance. We always seem to pass each other by, always moving in orbits and never properly colliding, don't you find?" I offered my hand.

L'Effroi briefly inspected the appendage as though he expected to see it holding a weapon, then he grasped it with gusto and pumped my arm in an overblown fashion, as though it should be clear to any onlookers that we had greeted one another. "Monsieur Pope! Such an unexpected surprise. I was led to believe you were unable to attend."

"Last minute change. Her Majesty can occasionally be fickle when deciding which of her many responsibilities are paramount in importance. One moment I'm to parley with the Prussians, the next I'm sent to soothe some obdurate Ottomans! But of course, you know how this goes." I felt sweat prickle my neck as it slipped down my collar.

"Yes, yes. It is such a shame we find ourselves on opposite sides of the table so often. From all that I hear about you I have always thought we might have more in common than the stances of our respective governments might suggest." Souriant was impressive. His features barely betrayed emotion while oozing good humour. He seemed perfectly relaxed.

"It is my hope that all you have heard is good, for me at least." We all chuckled politely. The lady's laughter was musical, without a hint of affectation.

"Now, gentlemen, I did not bring you together to talk shop…"

L'Effroi curled an eyebrow. "Oh, Madame? Then why would you? We are men of little else but our respective business."

"I would assume it was simply for the lady's own amusement, Monsieur." I offered, pinching a wry half-smile to my lips.

It was then that I felt it, like a caress inside my skull. It wasn't wholly unpleasant, but it was eerie. Mr Pope has instructed me in methods to shield my mind. It takes great concentration and detachment. It did not come naturally to me at all, but the basic premise was to think very surface thoughts. Alternatively, try to keep an abstract mind set, never fully letting full thoughts coalesce. Both terribly difficult to achieve under pressure! I found most success in the former, so I filled my mind with mundane observations, the most believable of which, in context of the moment, were appreciative thoughts regarding the lady.

This was no great chore. She was a delight in every way; beautiful, without being obvious or garish. Most impressive was her bearing. She moved so fluidly, each little mannerism as light as air, each gesture so compact but creating huge effect. She was utterly measured and in control, while every second she sent out suggestions that she held back so much more that you would never discover.

"You men play your games, some women like to set boards of their own. Let us call it a passing fancy. As you so aptly put it, Mr Pope, you travel in similar orbits but never seem to intersect. I wished to make that happen; a little social experiment. I find there is always a morbid curiosity in witnessing a collision." That smile again, lots of teeth, I couldn't be sure if she was insulting me or flirting.

The soft touch in my head intensified; there was a pressure pressing in on me. I wondered briefly if I only recognised it for what it was because I was forewarned. I then wondered if such thoughts would be clearly read and give me away?

The pressure was building as L'Effroi tried to dig further into my mind. I shuddered and knew within seconds I would cry out, when suddenly it stopped.

A man had approached Souriant and tapped him on the shoulder, breaking his concentration. He whispered into the spy's ear.

"Excuse me, a small matter has come to my attention. I will return presently. It is not for me to ruin the good madame's entertainment." He smiled a dazzling grin, turned with the click of his heels and went out towards a side corridor. I observed he did not leave the main hall, and made sure to position himself so he could watch me at all times.

The lady turned to me and offered her hand. "Shall we dance, Mr...?"

"You know who I'm not, I don't see why I should furnish you with more information. I don't believe I've had the pleasure of your name either," I parried.

"I get to be whomever I choose, Mr Jarvis. Tonight, I haven't decided if I am your master's friend, or otherwise."

We were moving about the floor in a gentle waltz. It was simple and easy, which I was thankful for as I felt at a constant disadvantage conversing with my dance partner. I very nearly tripped over when she used my proper name. I must admit to a private pleasure in dancing once again.

It then occurred to me that she had outmaneuvered me without any resistance at all. Mr Pope has never danced (as far as I am aware) in his life. He would certainly never be seen dancing. As we moved around the floor, I caught a few glances from long time diplomats and statesmen looking on as though they were witnessing something out of the ordinary. I tried to tell myself that they were simply admiring the lady, or at the very least wondering how on earth I had managed to win her hand for the turn.

"You have me at a total disadvantage, and have very neatly managed to give me away to anyone that might be observant enough. I might suggest, if you are not Mr Pope's enemy, you are not, at this moment, being much of an ally," I offered.

Thankfully the song ended. We stopped, bowed, and I led the lady from the floor. "It is useful to get some insight into the people that surround those that you must deal with. It is suggestive of how good their judgement is," she purred.

I spotted L'Effroi making his way back towards us, as the crowd parted before him. The lady leaned over to me and whispered, "In case you were wondering, the reason his mind probe was so uncomfortable was because it's never nice when two people are in one head at the same time." She winked. "You're welcome."

I coughed gently, trying to regain some measure of composure. "Monsieur Souriant, I do hope nothing troubling has come to your attention?" I asked.

His back stiffened a little. It was the first small break in his immaculate facade. "Nothing of any consequence, I'm sure, monsieur. Unless you know any better?"

"I'm not sure I quite take your meaning, sir!" I replied, adding a little spice of mock-offence.

He stepped in close to me and lowered his voice. I could smell the alcohol on his breath and feel the power pulsing in his body. I couldn't decide if it was purely physical, or an effect of his magical capabilities. "Yes you do, Pope. If you admit your game now, your accomplice will be spared. If you continue to play the fool, it will go harder for you both." He ended with a horrible smile, suggesting he might rather enjoy the latter.

A light pattering clap broke the tension. We both turned to see the lady applauding to herself and bouncing excitedly. "Oh my, I didn't think we'd get to this point quite so quickly. How wonderful." At the lightest touch on his shoulder from her, Souriant backed away. She moved in closer to him; she drifted like smoke.

"My good Monsieur Sourriant. If I may…" She reached a hand into her clutch bag. I was watching closely and I barely perceived the hand-off, but I was sure she passed a bundle of papers into the French spy's inside jacket pocket. "Those are most likely what an enemy agent is interested in, and they are now in your possession - as I promised they would be."

Souriant put a hand to his breast where the bundle of paper now lay. The lady drifted over to stand next to me. She lifted a hand and put it to my face. "And as much as I would have enjoyed a meeting between the two of you... I'm afraid I must tell you that this is not Silas Pope."

L'Effroi spluttered with the beginnings of rage.

"Did you really think *this* man could have been considered your equal in any way?" Souriant seemed a little mollified. "Think how disappointing that would have been; to finally meet the man, and realise he is so far beneath you. Where's the challenge?"

The lady rose onto her toes and gently laid a kiss upon my cheek. I felt her hand deposit something into my jacket pocket, but I was certain L'Effroi would not have seen it. I judged that people only saw what the lady allowed them to.

She moved back over to Souriant. "Now, I think first we shall dance, and then we must eat and drink until you are amply drunk enough to discuss my payment, and the extravagant bonus I am most certainly owed for keeping intact the rival that drives you to achieve so much." She tilted her head and looked directly into his eyes.

I once again felt the itch and prod within my skull as the two of them battled to read my mind. It left as quickly as it began.

Souriant smiled and then barked his raucous laugh. Without a backward glance to me, he escorted the lady to the dance floor and led a ferocious quickstep.

I was dumbfounded. It had not escaped me how close to harm, if not actual death, I had been. I had enough about me to notice that L'Effroi had nodded towards two security men on the other side of the hall, and they were making a line towards me.

I turned and made my way out of the grand hall. I wasn't certain what their orders might be. Perhaps it was simply to escort me out, maybe it would be an arrest and an interrogation, or perhaps they would simply kill me for the affront of trying to fool their master?

I made a few turns in the hallway. There were still a lot of people milling about. I could sense the security guards following me. They were gaining, and I didn't know the layout of the palace. I assumed they did.

As soon as the people loitering in the halls had thinned and then disappeared I broke into a trot. Turn after turn, the hallways became more sparse and narrow. I recognised that I was heading towards the service quarters, my usual domain. There would be a back entrance, or for my purposes, exit.

The feet of the security guards were heavy behind me. I came to a pair of double doors that were locked. I turned to face my fate, I reached into my sleeve for the concealed needle blade I had trained with. The guards ran towards me, confident of their victory.

Suddenly a door to the right of me opened, and a figure emerged placing themselves between the guards and me. I don't rightly know what happened, but the next thing my mind registered was the two guards in a heap on the floor, seemingly fast asleep, and Mr Pope was gently prising the blade from my grasp.

I don't recall very much after that.

It's so strange. As I write it all down, I feel the fear leaving me. The emotions are bland. Disconnected. I have the memories, but I no longer shudder or shrink from them.

I believe each time I undertake this simple process I gain a little more understanding of my master, and the sacrifices he endures.

I do feel better, but it leaves an emptiness; one I'm not certain will be filled again.

- - - - - - -

There was more movement outside the door I had entered through. I did have a cursory look at the windows. They were sealed and thick. We were also a fair way up, so that was not the most appealing plan. I was sure there might be a more elegant solution than blasting my way out and testing gravity. Though in a pinch I am not above such verbose actions, I like to think of myself as a more refined man of action.

I considered the doors again. It was far too odd to be an architectural quirk. Even these opulent palaces made by the order of crazed rulers rarely had such useless follies. In fact, if you looked at the building objectively, stripping away the facade of luxury, it had been built defensively. Large open spaces towards the front, smaller spaces at the back, lots of twisting hallways, easy to get turned around and lost. It was a functional design that gave an advantage to those that lived there and were familiar with it.

I turned my attention back to the two 'fake doors'. There was no gap around or under them; it was as though a regular door had been laid into mortar. The handle did not budge.

I couldn't spy any writing or markings on them. They were frustratingly 'normal' (I do so loathe using that word). I took a few different scrying stones from my inside pocket. I had learned through experience to look after them well. I held the first to my eye - it revealed nothing. The second gave me a hint of something. I decided to combine the holes of two stones and tried a third time, which revealed all.

I saw thin strands of light running from the frame of the door up into the ceiling and around the top of the room. They branched off here and there, some leading across to the other sealed door, but a group of them led around the room and descended again, aligning with a series of bell pull levers on the wall by the fireplace.

I hadn't noticed this oddity before. Of course, a bell pull is an ordinary mechanism in any large household, but there is only a need for one in any room. Here there was a group of them marked for various locations in the house. I translated the inscriptions: Billiards Room, Drawing Room, Service Corridor, Kitchens, Music Room, Master Suite, Front Door, amongst many of the usual locations you might expect, then oddest of them all… Gardens.

It clearly wasn't a regular bell pull system.

I felt a sudden fizzing of the atmosphere near the central door. The spell I had put on the lock to replace the one I had set off had been counteracted. I didn't take offence; it was a hasty effort at best, and I wasn't surprised that L'Effroi was able to disable it (at the time I didn't realise he'd managed it at such an impressive distance!). I heard a key being fit into the lock. I quickly moved towards the door, throwing some power towards the mechanism - heating and then cooling it rapidly to fuse it all into a solid block.

I heard a few expletives, the handle rattling and then the distinctive thumps of men attempting to break down a door.

I selected the 'Service Corridor' bell pull. It sounded like it would be towards the back of the palace, possibly near a service entrance/exit, and with any luck quite a long way from the party and security. I pulled the chord. I didn't need to look through my stones to perceive the magic - it could be clearly felt. There was a small flash of light around the edges of the door to the left of where I had entered, and a tiny movement as its weight settled on the hinges.

I went across, did a quick piece of due diligence to make sure I didn't set off any hidden traps, and tested the handle. The door swung easily into the room and beyond there was, as advertised, a sterile utilitarian corridor. As I closed the door I heard the one next to it creak and break as the men finally forced it open. As soon as the catch slid home, the door was once again sealed into the wall.

I didn't think there was an obvious way to tell which door I had taken, and didn't expect an immediate chase, but I also didn't want to take my chances. They would surely presume I had figured out their system, and begin trying doors to find me. I turned to complete my escape, when I was faced with two security guards running at me.

At first I was impressed that I had been tracked down so quickly, then I noticed that Jarvis was behind me, holding his blade ready to face the men.

I didn't particularly want to harm them so I put a trance field in front of them; as they passed through it they fell asleep before hitting the floor. I leant over them to whisper a few select words into their ears so they would forget the last few hours, and went to check on my attendant.

He was clearly in shock and very pliable - I simply took hold of him, and steered him along. To any observer it looked like a servant helping to usher his master discreetly out of the party after overindulging.

We passed through the kitchen, out into the back yard, and over the grounds to where the carriages were waiting to be called. I bundled Jarvis in, and away we went.

I will admit to giving a sigh of relief once we had crossed the threshold back into the city streets. I looked behind us for signs of pursuit, and found none.

Jarvis had a strange blank stare and he seemed to be uttering indecipherable words under his breath. All of a sudden he sat bolt upright, looked me dead in the eye with clarity, and produced a note from his jacket pocket. "From the lady," he proclaimed. Once I took it from him, he lapsed back into insensibility.

She had scented the paper. There would be no signature; she knew to me it would be obvious who had sent the note.

- - - - - - -

Silas, this evening was rather fun. Your man is so very interesting - I do believe he gives far too much away for you. Oh, and if all goes to plan you'll have to dance more at these things in the future.
I sold what you came here to acquire to L'Effroi. The French were willing to pay a lot of money for it. However, I'm never adverse to a little bonus payment.

*I have made copies, and would be happy to offer you
an excellent rate.*
*I hope your companion isn't too distressed. The games
we play do not suit most.*
Until next time… I do hope it is soon.
X

- - - - - - -

I closed my eyes and took in the scent one last time before
safely depositing the note in my jacket, next to the seeing stones.

We made it safely back to the British embassy, and indeed
all the way back to London without issue. The intelligence I
eventually received from Madame Durrant was effective in
changing the loyalties of the French in that particular matter,
so all was well, apart from Jarvis.

He was obviously shaken, and I knew the time had come
to sit him down with a Sentiment Stone and ensure he was
not permanently marked by the experience. His account of
the affair has made very interesting reading.

I never suspected that Madame Durrant had any magical
gifts at all, but it is clear she can, at least, interfere with a
powerful magician's ability to read minds. It is certainly
something to ponder.

As if I needed any more excuses for my thoughts to drift
towards Adrienne Durrant.

⚗︎⚗︎⚗︎⚗︎⚗︎⚗︎⚗︎⚗︎ ⚗︎⚗︎

It is some days since I last attempted to add to this exercise. Mr Hopkins did me a kindness; I was sedated and left in my room after my last attempt. He tells me I flew into a rage, and hysterics. I've read back what I wrote and I cannot fathom why it might have caused such distress. My feelings on those events have considerably evened out now. Mr Hopkins pointed to the stone I hold in my hand as the reason for it. He encouraged me to continue. Told me it would give me greater control over my emotions.

I must say, after my time in the insanitarium, even though the rooms are soft and comfortable, mastery of my feelings would be desirable.

The drawer in the bureau, that's where I'd got to. Yes. It was open. Inside I found an envelope addressed to me, containing a ring and a letter. It told me that I was free to take any and all books with me, but I absolutely must take the volumes and papers in the drawer where the letter was found. Turns out Mr Walton had an interest in magic. Not illusion, you understand, but real magic.

His books and papers contained instructional volumes as well as his own notes on experiments and the findings of certain investigations.

It all read like fantasy to me. Like the myths he enjoyed. But every time this thought came to me, the memory of the evening he died pricked my mind. I had witnessed evidence that there was something more. Something beyond the meat and bones of our world.

Following my habits, I began to read and learn as much as I could on the subject. New information was difficult to come by. I tried my best to work out how Mr Walton had begun his own occult education. A near lifetime of his own research had only filled a single drawer.

I wondered about Mr Walton's ring. It had a unique design, one that was repeated throughout his papers in reference to a private club or society. Including the ring in the letter suggested what might go on there. I wondered if I would be welcomed, as I had it. Perhaps members inducted new initiates by passing it on? I couldn't be sure, and I didn't want to risk making direct enquiries.

I was careful. I was patient.

I imagined Mr Walton had placed limits on what he was prepared to do to discover more about magic. There were bound to be unsavoury sources of information. It wasn't the sort of thing that you purchased for a penny on a street corner.

I, on the other hand, was happy to do things I shouldn't to find out more.

I'd always thought it was only rich gentlemen who formed secret societies. The group I had stumbled over through Mr Walton seemed to include a wide range of society. The papers included a members' list and charter. I wanted to find out more about these men (in fact, there were a few women too, which surprised me), before a direct approach.

I had it in my head that Mr Walton was supposed to pass all this on, and I would be welcomed. But I couldn't help thinking he was doing something wrong, and I would be punished for his actions.

For a few weeks I followed some of the other members. I was discrete. I happened to be in the places they regularly went, or I made introductions looking for more work, giving my time helping Mr Walton as a reference, of sorts.

A few of the members lived close by. I tried travelling to find others, but my time was limited. In the end I did my best to involve myself in the lives of those close at hand.

I managed to pick up a bit of work as a scribe for one of the other members - Mr Furlong. He was a local landlord that took a very hands-on approach to his work. He was always in need of someone to write letters by dictation. He wasn't a rich gent, but certainly a hard working businessman. He wore his ring openly. I asked him about it once and he dismissed it as a frippery, though I felt his gaze linger on me after I turned away.

It unnerved me when Mr Furlong approached me directly and asked about Mr Walton's papers and ring. He knew perfectly well that I had them. I didn't see any sense in denying it.

I was welcomed into the society. It turned out that my initial assumption was correct. Members passed on their place to a person of their choosing to be apprenticed by someone else. It is part of the initiation, to see how the recipient reacts. I had been watched from the moment I discovered Mr Walton's papers.

Seemingly, I had impressed them.

I was officially an initiate within The Order of the Inner Dawn; a society that studied occult literature, with little interest in the practicalities of what they read.

It was everything I wanted, and more.

We met once a week to present papers on aspects of natural and chemical magic, as well as occult scripture.

THE JOURNAL OF SILAS POPE

The Order had an extensive library, which I did my best to consume in its entirety.

If I had any spare time it was spent in the library.

Unfortunately, shortly after I had begun my magical education, my free time became very limited.

My mother fell ill.

This is where things began--

This is when I made my mistake--

I first heard the name of 'The Amazing Thaddeus Volk: Master Magician' a few years before he came to significant prominence. It is part of my BOSS duties to attempt to keep track of magical practitioners. It is impossible to record a strict register, and it would risk lapsing into draconian measures to suggest something formal, not to mention impossible to enforce with the resources at our disposal. Like most governmental departments (for that is what we are, even though there is a tacit agreement between Parliament and Her Majesty that the Queen continues to oversee us) we are stretched, and have to make do dealing with the biggest threats and hoping the smaller ones do not develop in directions that require our attention. Even so, I try my damnedest to keep an eye on any practitioners of note so I can identify possible threats early.

To this end, and as odd as it seems, more variety performers than you might imagine are, in fact, using real magic instead of perpetrating illusion. It is a bugbear of mine; I find it vulgar and lazy. There is actually more artistry in developing a skill for slight of hand or engineering clever devices than using proper magic for frippery and fame.

Some of those in my immediate circle have mistaken my interest in the theatre for leisure. I never correct an inaccurate assumption. It is much better for anyone aspiring to be a spy to constantly assess their own conclusions. Any agent or recruits that try to curry my favour with talk of the West End or tickets to a show are noted for their poor judgement.

Thaddeus Volk was a minor footnote in my hurried investigations. He barely registered at all. His act was rather run-of-the-mill. Any hints of actual magic were a little disheartening, as the effects they achieved could have just as easily been done with conventional, non-powered methods. I dismissed him as low skilled and lacklustre. I imagined he would only ever present a threat to himself by testing the powers he had too far through indolence.

Bearing this in mind, I was somewhat taken aback to find a large advert for his latest show in The Times. I filed this piece of information away in my mind, but I never expected to give it any serious thought. He had obviously found an excellent publicist, or a benefactor with no taste and deep pockets.

I managed to forget all about 'The Amazing Volk' once again, until his show had been running for a week or so. Word of it spread like wildfire around the city. It was the hottest ticket to be had.

A strong note of confusion was added to my earlier surprise.

Could it be that I had fallen victim to being too trusting of my own assumptions? Had I missed something about the performer's character; his potential?

Unfortunately I would have to see the show to find out. Actually, I would have to see it twice.

I had only skimmed the advert in The Times and neglected to register the venues that were listed. That's correct - 'venues', plural. Volk's show began in the New Prince's Theatre on Shaftsbury Avenue and was completed in the Winter Garden Theatre on Drury Lane, then for his finale he would make an appearance in Covent Garden. I'm sure you can imagine, on the face of things, it is a very strange arrangement. Until you understand the nature of his trick.

Volk would perform his act (from initial reports it sounded perfectly ordinary) at the New Prince's, then at the interval he would thank the audience and joke that he had another show to attend. He would walk through a door and frame set in the middle of the stage, disappear in a puff of smoke, and reappear through a similar door on the stage of the Winter Garden to rapturous applause from a second audience. He would then repeat his act. As a finale he would once again disappear though the door and reappear through a third door placed in Covent Garden, in full view of the public.

It had taken a few performances for the audience to realise what was happening. On first impressions it was a simple disappearing trick. The first audience didn't get to appreciate the reappearance. After a few nights the press began to get curious; they stationed reporters at each theatre, and sent runners and spotters between the venues. They wanted to see if they could beat the magician across the near half-mile distance. They also wanted to keep watch to see if the performer could be seen making the journey by physical means. Needless to say, Volk had always appeared and begun his second performance before the runner made it to the Winter Garden, and nobody had seen the magician on London's streets between the theatres.

The same was done between the Winter and Covent Gardens. Again, Volk emerged unflustered from the door to an increasingly large and loud crowd of observers.

Over a week or so this trick became a thing of legend. Volk did indeed have an excellent (and expensive) publicist that stirred and funnelled the interest of the audience and press alike. Together they concocted all sorts of tests and stunts to show how miraculous it all was.

The streets were cleared each evening for running races to take place between the venues. The fittest, fastest men came to take the challenge and try to beat the conjuror across town. They even tried a sprint relay to cover the ground in the fastest way possible. This graduated to carriages and horse races along the roads, with each participant desperate to cover the distance quicker than Volk. All to no avail. The seemingly 'Master Magician' never failed.

Theories abounded. There was talk of secret underground tunnels, body doubles, even appeals to look in the birth registry as some reporters were convinced they were being hoodwinked by twins.

Just as many wanted to keep the magic intact, not wanting it to be explained, revelling in the wonder of something that seemed utterly impossible.

A city watchmaker was drafted into the publicity circus. The most expensive and accurate mechanical movement they made was set up at each venue, surrounded by crowds and reporters. The precise minute and second of each disappearance and reappearance would be noted every night, then reported each morning. It was always an interval of around a minute. Column inches were filled with the significance of a second or two either side of the average.

It became a sensation. The run of shows was only scheduled to be three weeks. There was public demand and outcry for an extension; a ticket simply could not be purchased honestly. Volk stayed away from the press - his publicist handled all promotion. This gave the performer a further air of mystery.

It was said the trick drained his mental and spiritual energies; he needed rest and meditation to be able to perform each night, for if he was not properly refreshed the trick would pull him apart or land him in an otherworldly realm, trapped and never able to return.

The second and third hand ticket markets were all being run by the theatres and the act's management. The money changing hands was obscene.

That was the only part of it that gave me pause on my initial investigations. For investigate I did. I simply had to. If Volk was indeed employing magic of this magnitude, his skills had taken a great leap and would need to be noted and assessed.

I managed to get a ticket on consecutive nights. I certainly didn't pay the going rate. We may not be the most highly funded of Her Majesty's agencies, but our connections run deeply through all strata of society. Knowing the correct people is often more than half the battle.

In fact, I gave three evenings of my life to this episode, two of which I had to endure Volk's performances. I was rather relived on the first night, as I came to the conclusion that my original assessment of Thaddeus Volk was not too wide of the mark. He was still lazy and sloppy; he cut corners that wouldn't have needed to be cut with very little application. I sensed small bursts of proper craft here and there, but nothing that raised alarm.

The crowd were delighted by it all. I wept for common sense to prevail. Hundreds of them, like sheep, had been convinced they were witnessing genius.

Then came the finale. A very ordinary door and frame was raised upon the stage. Volk prattled on, laying the risks of his trick on thick, and then he walked through and was gone. I felt a very strong pulse of power but it was untidy.

It is a difficult thing to explain. Magic is like handwriting; you can shape it to function as you wish, but it can be messy... sloppily rendered. That was the case with Volk. He had learned a real trick, something quite impressive, but he had not taken the time to properly refine it. There was something else about it too. It didn't feel like the work of a single practitioner. There was a flourish at the root of it with the hasty formation of Volk tacked on.

My guess was that the trick was not the magician's originally, it was something that had been gifted to him and he had tried to make it his own.

I had heard of similar feats being gifted from teacher to student, usually when they were near death. It is an inheritance of power, usually a specific spell or function. My guess was that somebody had gone to a lot of trouble to make Mr Volk a star performer, but I wasn't convinced that was the sum total of the motivation. The profits were clear to see in ticket sales and general attention, however if you had the ability to pull the trick off why not simply do it yourself? A choice had been made to elevate a low level performer and offer them a career making turn.

It nagged at me. There must have been more to it.

The crowd raced from their seats. It had become habit, for most, to make the journey over to the Winter Garden where an usher would confirm the success of the trick to a crowd that waited outside. They would then wander to Covent Garden and await the finale.

I was the last to leave my seat. I went up on stage after showing my credentials to the theatre staff. The door and frame were unremarkable. I had used doors to traverse distance before, but it took the rendering of sigils and markings into the wood itself to take effect. What was on stage was a simple prop. I observed that it was placed in front of a trapdoor. I went off stage to find my way below. Everything the audience saw was artifice. A small smoke bomb, and the performer drops from view. The real magic happened once the first illusion was complete.

The darkness under the stage was intense, with slices of light beaming through cracks between the planks above. I studied the latch on the trapdoor; it was spring loaded, so it would open under pressure and then replace itself. Again, no magic. A musty break-fall pillow lay beneath the trapdoor. There must have been someone here to pull the latch on the door. I wondered if they were also under here to witness the real trick. I could taste the energy of the power in the enclosed space - it had a coppery tang, mixed with salt.

There was nothing else to see. I expected some accoutrements, some physical materials to aid the magic. Possibly even a sacrifice. That could only mean that the spell was wholly performed internally, which increased the difficulty and, I must admit, the meagre respect I carried for Volk up to that point. Even with help, full bodily travel from one place to another is a power of the highest order; something I have never been able to master, not that I am the general measurement of power, of course.

Having confirmed the nature of the magic, or at least finding no evidence to suggest a simpler method, it helped to guide my thinking. There were limitations to magical travel. There are all sorts of problems with line of sight and distance. Magic does not cover all bases; if you get it wrong, you can re-emerge in the middle of a wall, or in solid soil if you judge the ground levels incorrectly.

I left the theatre and began to wander along the streets towards the Winter Garden. The crowds and fuss had moved on, so there was just the usual bustle and buzz about the West End, all undercut by the hiss of the gas lamps and the constant trickle of water in the drains, even when it hadn't rained.

I walked a zigzag route through the side streets and alleyways between the main thoroughfares. It is not generally recommended to do so late at night in the city. I must admit I would have preferred not to, even when I had nothing to fear from the people that inhabit such places. Whores and robbers use the low light and relative privacy to ply their trades, both taking advantage of the drunks that stumble through the darkness.

I ignored all but the slope of the streets and the positions of the buildings. I was doing my best to understand how the city was composed between where Volk disappeared and where he reappeared. Of course, I couldn't confirm precisely where he appeared until I inspected the Winter Garden. The only time I took note of people in these back streets was when I encountered some, like me, that seemed to have no business being there. They were heavily built and had very obvious concealed weapons about their persons.

I didn't bother to go all of the way to the second venue. I had made my observations, and I noted a few questions to look into the next day before attending the second performance.

The newspapers were full of the same sensationalism, and the streets were abuzz with little else as I headed back to the alleys between the two theatres. Daylight cast a different pall on the environment, which was without doubt dirty, but minus the people much less sinister. I made the journey to confirm that the burly men, or at least some burly men (I didn't bother to note if they were the same men), were still stationed outside the nondescript building I had come upon hours previously.

I sent runners to a few civil servants that owned me favours, and got the answers I expected. I was beginning to warm to my task.

The performance that evening at least had the added bonus of beginning well, as Volk transported himself onto stage. Again, all was masked with smoke; I assumed the same theatrics were at play in this venue. I had a seat closer to the stage, which gave me a better view of the man. He performed well enough - there was a smile and flourish to his motions, but below it all I spotted a strain.

The show ended with an exit as showy as the entrance, as Volk headed off to his public in Covent Garden. I had asked Jarvis to attend the public reappearance and make a note of the time. I was sure to check my own watch as the magician made his exit. After my walk earlier in the day and the fog of it all beginning to clear, I had a small detail I wished to check. Oddly, the press had only made a fuss about the time that elapsed between Volk's travel between the venues. That seemed to be the test, in their eyes; the final hop was seen as an extravagance and not as ardently scrutinised.

Once again I went below the stage. It was much the same as the New Prince's - the same smells and feelings. The same setup, though this time there was a simple set of steps to ascend to the trapdoor, which was later swapped with a break-fall.

There was one curious addition. A small safe sat beneath the stage. It was bolted and chained to the floor, and the door was slightly ajar. It was empty.

I went along the streets doing a similar sweep of alleyways and side-roads, towards Covent Garden to meet Jarvis. I often stopped to take my bearings and distinguish line of sight back to the Winter Garden. I had memorised a map of the area earlier in the day, and identified a premises that fitted my working theory. I kept my distance and surveilled. I was wholly unsurprised to find another set of armed guards, but these ones were of a much rougher sort.

I slipped away and found Jarvis, who reported his observations to me. We compared timings and found that Volk took three minutes to make the trip from his last venue to the public reappearance. It might have seemed like an insignificance, but to me it was confirmation. I would only have liked to find out if that timing had been growing over the course of the run of shows.

I asked Jarvis what he thought of 'The Amazing Thaddeus Volk' and his answer was unequivocal: "He seemed like a very unwell man putting on a brave face to me, sir."

That night I sent out a note to the head of security at Bearings Bank. We had a fruitful discussion that allowed me access to one of their secret vaults. It happened to lie in an unassuming backstreet between Shaftsbury Avenue and Drury Lane.

I waited in the darkness, keeping time in my head, imagining the progress of the show happening a few streets away. I recalled each trick and gesture; as I imagined Volk falling through the stage behind his smoke, I braced myself for action.

I felt the pulse of energy before the magician appeared. It was strange, and I wished for more light to see it properly. As it was, I knew the man was in the vault by his heavy breathing and the stench of his sweat mixed with the profuse amount of perfume he used to mask it.

I kept silent, wanting to confirm my suspicions in person before revealing myself. As I guessed, Volk was carrying something heavy in a cloth; he unwrapped what looked like a gold bar, then swapped it with one from the large pile of gold in the centre of the vault.

Just as Volk was re-wrapping what he had taken, I stood and sent a pulse of power towards him. It stiffened his muscles, forcing him to stay perfectly still. "Thaddeus Volk, in the name of Her Majesty the Queen I place you under arrest for misuse of magical power," I said.

A wave of magic stirred. He didn't need motion to summon the spell that would transport him. I took up my stick ready to strike when the surge subsided, and Volk lost consciousness. It is a strange sight to see someone pass out while not being able to move a muscle. Even so, I thought I caught a look of relief in his eyes as they drooped closed.

In a more traditional manner I transported Mr Volk back to BOSS HQ, and let him rest in one of our void field cells. They are most uncomfortable places for practitioners to be. I do not like using them, but it is the only way we can properly control or punish magic users that go awry.

That same night as I was capturing Volk I sent a team to the address between Drury Lane and Covent Garden. They overcame the criminal guards, known associates of the 'Hallem Mews Gang' - an emerging power in the northern slums of the city. To everyone's surprise but mine they discovered and recovered a large cache of gold bars.

I wished to question Volk as soon as he regained consciousness, but he never did. He died that very same night.

It cannot be confirmed for sure, but I believe it is clear Mr Volk had been hired by a very powerful magician who gifted him the ability to transport himself bodily across a considerable distance with great accuracy. He had been chosen as a low level performer who had been chasing fame for years without success. It seemed likely he would jump at the chance to become an overnight sensation.

Sadly, Thaddeus Volk was not the primary perpetrator of this crime. He was also a victim. The power that was gifted to him was consuming his life force each time he used it. It is a great power that should only ever be used sparingly, or with long recovery time in between uses. It was never meant for such regular journeys. Volk was jumping four times a night for nearly a fortnight; I'm unsure if he would have been able to endure the full three-week run as planned.

It was one of the most elegant bank robberies I have ever witnessed. Bearings Bank held the gold in a small store for a short time. I have yet to get to the bottom of how the information was obtained by whoever was pulling Volk's strings. The magician would take a steel bar painted gold on his first jump to the vault, and swap his fake for a real one before jumping to the second theatre. Here he would store the gold in the safe below stage while he did the second performance, then collect it as he jumped to the storage house between Drury Lane and Covent Garden. His final jump would be the public reappearance to take his very well earned applause.

The time differential bothered me to begin with. Without a stop the journey would be instantaneous. The growing time difference on the final jump was telling in that the trick was taking a physical toll on the performer. He needed a little more time to recover.

Bearings were very grateful for the recovery of the gold. They secretly confided in me that the loss would have surely taken them under if it had not been caught.

I write this account to rid myself of the gnawing doubt I have in my gut. I caught someone doing wrong, but in a way Thaddeus Volk was as much a victim as the bank might have been. Of course, now the man is a legend. He never did appear upon the Winter Garden stage that fateful night, and he will never be seen again. The publicist has spun his tale, warning audiences of the dangers his acts face to delight and entertain them. It will be a mystery that will last through the ages and Volk will be remembered as one of the great magical performers of the age. I wonder if he might have taken this result if it was offered to him? I think he probably might have done. Perhaps he knew the cost? It almost makes me feel sad for the man. Perhaps he got what he deserved?

I must find out who is behind all of this. The great power inside Volk has died with him. I do not believe for a moment that whomever gifted it to him did not plan to take it back once the heist was complete. Perhaps I should have waited longer and let it play out to catch the mastermind? The Hallem Mews Gang may provide leads in that direction, but that is for another day.

I cannot help but think of the adulation Volk received for his efforts. I wonder how dangerous I might become if I ever craved it?

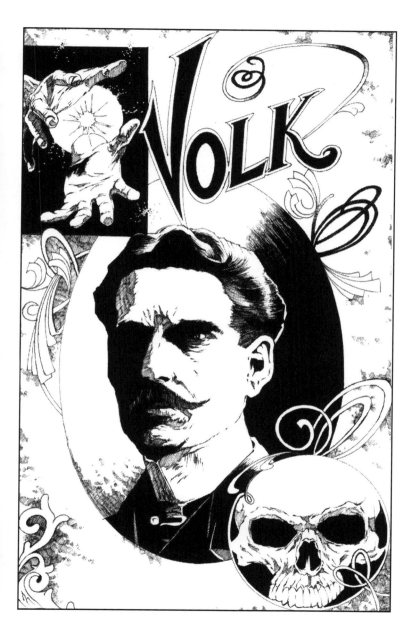

CHAPTER 9

Mr Hopkins tells me he cannot give me more time. If he is to take me under his wing, as he would wish, I need to be stable enough to leave this wretched, padded room. Until I can speak about my parents without ill effects I won't be allowed to leave.

He said I should begin by baldly stating the facts. Quickly, and in few words. It will take the main sting from my recollections. It will help me.

I am the reason my parents are dead.

I killed them.

I am alone.

I have seen Hell.

I have battled one of its beasts.

I am alive.

I wish I wasn't.

9

⚡ 𝔅𝔦𝔫𝔞𝔩𝔢𝔤𝔤𝔶 𝔦𝔦𝔦

Ancient stories were passed between people before there was a method to record them. They were called the Dark Ages for very good reason. But the tales endured. It can be assured that they changed significantly through the centuries of retellings. Some parts might have been misremembered, others changed by overdramatic orators. In a way, each of us holds a different story in our heads, even though we might have heard the same recitation or read the same text.

The central parts of any story are immutable; the bones of it. Anything outside of that is probably fair game for change. Bearing all this in mind, I always assumed the big legends were formulated by people that had misunderstood the nature of the things they had seen, and had to create a story to process it - make sense of it.

The majority of the public have no idea about the true nature of the world even now, so imagine a mortal thousands of years ago meeting a Grindylow or a Hulder, even a witch. You would see things that were impossible to explain to others. You'd do your best though. That story would grow, deepen, and become quite unrecognisable from how it began.

I imagined the biggest legends had humble beginnings that had been vastly overblown. Until I met one in person.

I'll admit to being relieved to leave London in the immediate aftermath of the great storm, as the newspapers were calling it. Those in the know called it the battle of the

Naiads. The spirit of the River Thames had been killed, but she had taken the invading Rhinedaughter (who had tainted the major waterways of the nation) with her. The threat of a new spirit controlling the Thames had passed, but so had the protection of the original power.

The spoiled water had spread disease nationwide. It was being reported as cholera, and most blamed it on 'bad air' or poor hygiene. It was down to the water, and every person, rich or poor, relied on a supply of water.

The death toll was beyond reckoning, and without river spirits to cleanse the disease there was no solution. No hope.

Mother Thames had left me with a parting instruction-rather an order. If she should perish I must go to seek the help of the Lady in the Lake; Nimue Viviane. She was the only sorcerer in the realm that had the power to rebalance nature.

I thought I'd long given up being surprised in this line of work, but finding that a figure from ancient lore might actually exist today was humbling. If I did find her and she really had endured through time, what else might have survived? What else might actually be history rather than legend?

Typically, Mother Thames had not furnished me with some convenient map co-ordinates to make the task simple! I had spent days in the BOSS archives reading everything we had on Arthurian legends. I went through the medieval texts we held, the French romances, I re-read Mallory and Walter Scott's relatively modern poem. There was not much to go on to bring these legends into reality.

Over the years it seemed I had not been the only BOSS agent to wonder how much of legend might be fact. There were incomplete investigations into possible real world locations for sites in the stories. I trusted a conclusion of my predecessor that the Isle of Avalon could really only be one place in England.

Which is why I found myself in Glastonbury. Centuries past, the famous Glastonbury Tor was a hill surrounded by a large lake. There was only one point of access, making it the perfect geological location for a defensible fort. As the years passed the lands changed, but the legend had been cast, and as I looked up at the Tor from a distance it struck me that the land yet remembered its history.

There was no longer a lake around the hill. It was flat farm and marshland. Due to the unique atmospherics there appeared to be a constant haze at the base of the hill, where the damp rising from the land met the dry air. It looked very much like a lake to me. As I've stated before, I don't hold with the idea of coincidence.

I had decided to undertake this mission alone. Jenkins had survived the ordeal on the Thames, and it had convinced him that a quieter life spending more time with his family would be a sensible choice. I envied him a little, that he could make such a choice.

The only real difficulty, or perhaps discomfort, was making sure I had clean water. For weeks I had taken to boiling and cooling all water that I consumed. The further out into the country I got, the more likely it was that the waterways were unaffected, but it was not a risk I could afford to take.

I made for what had been dubbed 'The Perilous Bridge'. I raised an eyebrow at that name, briefly wondering if the Fae had any involvement with the old tales. Perhaps a perilous bridge might lead into the perilous realm? The Lady Morgana, from the tales, certainly fitted that bill. I proceeded with caution.

Looking towards the Tor, there was a layer of mist separating us. It was so thick I felt as though I might be able to walk across it. No land could be seen through it, or even beyond it. The sky was grey too; the world felt like it had closed about me. Ahead the monolithic hill, with a tower stood atop it like a single broken tooth protruding from a gum.

I was at a loss to know what I should do. I believed I had found the place, and while there was no lake, the landscape was doing an impressive imitation of one.

I reached out with my senses. I did not utter a word, but projected my thoughts out across the landscape. "I have been sent by Mother Thames to seek Nimue Viviane. She has perished, and believed you to be the only being in this land that might heal the ills that have befallen it." I kneeled, because when dealing with entities of superior and unknown powers, a bit of deference never hurts.

The mist and fog began to move slowly in threads; there was a flow that had not been there before. The air was still but the fog wrapped around me in a silent and languid vortex. I was in the epicentre of an atmospheric tube. I looked up to see the sky, but its colour merged with the mists to make the difference imperceptible. The tube shifted and flowed down to a horizontal angle, changing from a column into a tunnel. A passageway.

I was very aware that the direction of the tunnel led straight off the side of the bridge I had been standing upon. There was no solid ground where it led. It felt like a test. I stepped up onto the bridge parapet, put my foot out onto the fog and trusted to the power that was extending me this invitation.

I promptly fell from the bridge through the mists into the small stream below. It took a split second for me to realise that I had not hit the bottom. It was a shallow stream that should have barely come up to my waist, yet I was still falling. Then the fall began to feel different; I stopped moving due to my downward momentum, and began to be pulled down. My lungs were burning. At any moment my body would instinctively try to inhale, and I would drown. My desperation began to mount. I had no control, and struggling would do no good. I gave in. As I was about to take a lungful of water, a light appeared below me; I was being pulled towards it.

Then I broke the surface.

I had not been pulled to the bottom, but forced to a different top. I heaved in huge gasps of air. The panic I had experienced was slow to drain away. I was alive, but danger felt imminent. Then I realised I wasn't treading water, or even floating - a force was holding me comfortably in the water. It was calming. My head was above the water, and my body was relaxed, held by gentle eddies and currents that were not naturally occurring. They were soft, almost playful, but I couldn't help feeling they could be used with force or for restraint if necessary.

I looked around. I was indeed in a vast lake. A bridge was above me, but it was very different from the small structure I had fallen from. It was the same location; my view of the Tor across the water was unchanged except for the structure atop it. A thin mist clung to the lake, and there were ethereal lights glowing all around.

A whirlpool began to twist in the water a few feet in front of me. It was strange, as the corkscrew flow was travelling up not flowing down. It was also very slow. A robed head emerged from the centre of the vortex, and rose until a figure was stood in the natural eddy. The water receded into a bowl so deep that we were facing one another at a similar height, even though just my head was above the surface.

Slender fingers adorned by jewelled rings drew back the hood of the robe. The face of a beautiful young woman was revealed. It was slender, but not sharp. Her mouth naturally fell to a slight smile, and her hair was a deep green inlaid with stones and garlands of water plants. The eyes betrayed her appearance. There was a depth to them that told of long ages and vast knowledge.

"Welcome, Silas Pope. I am Nimue, and this is my realm. I will hear the message you bring, but I will not guarantee my aid."

The tone was friendly enough, though everything else about the situation said so much more. I was being held in a place and a situation where it was very clear my life was completely in the lady's hands.

I bowed my head as best I could by submerging my mouth into the water and closing my eyes. "I thank you for passage to your lands, my lady. I cannot pretend to understand the journey or the destination, but I am happy to give over my life to your will. I mean no harm to you or this place."

Nimue nodded. The water around me swirled, and the pressure it applied to my body lessened. A bowl in the water was carved out for me, down to my chest. I was still being held, but I was being showed a bare minimum of trust. "Very well, Mr Pope. Please say your piece."

I told the tale of the Rhinedaughter coming to the kingdom's shores; how she stayed and usurped her way across the waters of the land, gaining power and leaving a trail of disease until she was ready to challenge the spirit of the River Thames. They battled to the death, both spirits diminishing, leaving the water ruined and no way for nature to rebalance the great cost of the river wars.

Throughout the telling the Lady Nimue seemed unmoved - bored, in fact. I wasn't certain that the troubles of the mortal world reached her concerns.

"Mother Thames was quite right to direct you toward me. I believe I may be able to help. The Naiads can be renewed; while they are not of my creation, I am able to replenish the natural powers if they fail or err. But I will not do this thing lightly." She looked at me, and I felt as though her gaze saw me completely. "You are a practitioner of magic, you understand the basic principles of exchange. Each time we use our power something is taken from us. This act would greatly drain me.

"I will need something in return." She smiled a smile that didn't reach her eyes, and made me feel how cold the water was.

"I'm not sure what is within my power that might be of use to you, my lady?" I replied, genuinely perplexed and not a little worried.

"I will not lie, the task I have in mind will cost you much, though you may not feel it immediately. I wish you to accept a curse that lies in wait for me, so you might retrieve something I deem precious. In return I will lend you my daughters who can bring balance to your damaged rivers until such a time as the Naiads re-emerge to take control once again."

I didn't feel as though a choice was being presented to me. I wondered what would happen if I decided that I wasn't prepared to take her quest? The reality of the situation was that I had come seeking help, and I was prepared to do anything to save my country further harm. It is the very definition of my job to take great personal risks for the good of those that will never know of them.

I told the Lady of the Lake that she had my service.

Suddenly I was once again on dry land. The water had lifted me as a liquid tentacle, and placed me on the bridge. I realised just how restricted I had been only once I was free of the water. It was the most subtle prison I had ever been in.

The lady was still in her whirling bowl of water, now looking up at me. "I will send my first daughter Ganieda as your guide. If you do all she asks I will heal your land." She had no need to make any suggestions of what might happen if I refused or failed. "I will not wish you good fortune, for this task has none, but I will spare hope for your fortitude." With that she let the waters once again claim her. The vortex ended, and the surface was still.

Out of the mists to my left a shape coalesced. I couldn't be sure if the figure was moving through the fog or being made by it. The young woman that came into view was strikingly similar to the lady in the water, similar dress and robes, though her hair was fiery red and she lacked the weight of history behind her eyes. She held her right hand up in passive greeting, and smiled benevolently.

"I'm sure you have many questions, and they are all quite needless. I will do my best to explain, but I suspect you will not get any answers that will make you feel any better." Ganieda's voice was bright and sparkling, like a gentle waterfall in a secluded glade. "Do you need rest or refreshment before we begin our journey? It is not far but it will exert a toll upon you. The paths we must take are not kind to mortals."

I was exhausted. It was only then becoming clear that my dive into the stream had been more taxing than I had realised, but I did not want to stay in that place. I felt a pressure in the atmosphere. I would be unwelcome until I completed my mission.

"I think we should make a start. Will there be places to rest along the way?" I asked.

"Yes, that might be possible," she smiled, reading my thoughts. "Mother is much warmer once you get to know her." Then she laughed, and the air around us brightened. "Follow me, I know where you might take some rest."

I followed her across the bridge and into the mists. Lights danced in the distance, though my depth perception was nil - they could have been tiny pinpricks of light very close. Tunnels in the fog like the one that had begun my journey from the original bridge opened all around us as we moved.

Ganieda signalled with her hand which one we would be taking. She walked with her feet obscured by mist. I couldn't see beneath it. She laughed when I tentatively tested the ground to make sure I was not heading for another surprise fall.

"No tests of faith now, Mr Pope. You have passed, and will be allowed to walk these tunnels as long as I guide you."

That gave me enough confidence to take a few steps, and once I stopped thinking about what I was actually placing my feet upon, I accepted that it didn't really matter.

I did briefly worry about how many times I had been forced to give up any sort of control I had to the environs I found myself in, and simply believe that they would support me or allow me to exist within them. Oddly, none of these places felt particularly unnatural, they were simply more guarded or protective of themselves than the relatively passive nature mortals enjoy in our own world. For I was sure that I was travelling through places utterly removed from my usual existence.

The lights flickered on and off. Sometimes I felt they were close, other times I knew they were distant - I can't explain how. In front of us a large light was sustained, and grew as we walked. Then the mists cleared and we were stood upon a small hill next to a church. We were surrounded by gravestones, and in front of us was a large and imposing rock. It didn't seem to mark a grave; it was simply part of the geology. It had been there long before the church, and I wondered how there were graves so close to it, as surely they would have been impossible to dig.

Ganieda pointed towards the rock. "We will rest here for a short while. I think it best that I tell you a tale related to your task, and then I will try to answer some of the questions you are bound to have."

I gratefully took a seat in the grass; it was dry and smelled sweet. I fished in my haversack for a skin of water and a small pan. "May I light a fire?" I asked.

The daughter of the lake smiled and nodded, herself taking a seat close by.

I gathered some scrub and cupped my hand about it to start a small fire. First there was smoke, then a tentative flame. I fed it some of the dry grass, and soon there was a fire. I had put a stone in the middle of my fuel and sat my pan upon it to boil some water.

After all of this, Ganieda handed a flask to me. "This water is untainted if you wish for refreshment?"

I barked a harsh laugh. "Why did you watch me go through all of that, when you were going to freely offer what I was trying to make?"

"Because mortals fascinate me... so industrious, so adaptable. You didn't think to ask me if I had what you needed, you were too focused on looking after yourself. I guess you would have shared what you made with me too?" said Ganieda

"Of course," I replied.

"Self-sufficiency and generosity; two of the most laudable traits in your kind. I wanted to see them for myself."

"Well, now I've got the fire going I'll boil some up anyway. It'll keep until later," I replied a little tersely, feeling like a subject of study.

I sipped the water from the flask - it was clean and refreshing. I took some hard biscuit from my bag and crunched on it; it would not satisfy appetite, but it would do well to battle hunger. I offered, but the lady wisely refused.

"You know the old tales, I've no doubt. The fact that you knew where you might find my mother proves this. So I will tell you a story you are familiar with, but it is the true version, or rather our version, not yours. Maybe the truth lies somewhere between them?

"My mother Nimue was once a student of a great sorcerer. He was famed throughout the land; an advisor to kings, the power behind the throne of many. He took students now and again, and it seemed to be part of his practice that his apprentices would also become his lovers. The gender did not matter to him - his game was one of power and influence.

"None of the students did anything against their will, but they endured much in exchange for what they learned. My mother learned contempt.

"She learned all she could from the wizard. She was his best student, his most willing lover. She wanted to make sure all of his secrets were laid bare to her so that she might one day be his match, even try to best him.

"The wizard had the power of foresight and knew his student's mind. He knew his peril, but such was his infatuation he accepted it gladly.

"My mother has often pondered that her teacher accepted his fate as a form of penance. That he realised he had abused his power and needed time to consider his actions. Nevertheless, my mother made her plans. She was his constant companion, and only when she was sure there was nothing more to learn from her teacher she lured him to a cave and sealed him within it.

"She set herself as judge and jury upon him, the only person capable of it as she became his equal. She did not trust his judgement because of the way he had treated his students. A man with such immense power, who took advantage of his position, could do wrong to so many.

"Nimue swore that she could and would do better. She became advisor to the king, and played the role at court. Even though she knew in her heart that her actions were true, in moments of self doubt she would visit her teacher; to judge if he could change, to consider releasing him. Alas, each time he saw her his obsession intensified. He had great power, but was overcome by his mortal urges.

"My mother never had that problem, she was half Fae. She used her wiles to her advantage on the weak-willed, but never let her mortal emotions control her. The only facets of her mortality that she nurtured were those of justice and care.

"She knew she would never be able to release the wizard, so long after her function as the great king's advisor she sealed the cave forever with a powerful heirloom of that court. She told her teacher what she intended to do, and gave him a choice; remain here forever as you are, alone, or forsake your power and choose the weaknesses of your mortality, and die.

"Your quest is to unseal that cave to reclaim the ancient heirloom. For my mother to ask this, she must be certain that her former teacher finally made the compassionate choice."

I had been lost in the tale. It was at once familiar and new. The fresh perspective and nuance had me enthralled. The enormity of its meaning was temporarily lost on me. When I realised the implications I nearly choked on my biscuit.

"Why don't you use names, my lady? For surely you talk of Merlin the wizard, and Arthur the great king?"

She smiled. "Of course, yes, they are whom I speak of. I find when we strip away names from the stories that we think are connected to them, their places in the tale become more human, their actions more relatable.

"If I told you straight away you might be tasked with releasing the great Merlin from his prison, would you still be sitting here?"

I considered this. "Yes, very probably, but I'm a foolish man hoping to save his own land. There is very little I won't consider doing."

"An excellent answer. You will need this conviction, for no matter what, whether he is alive or dead, the person that opens the prison will be susceptible to harm. Either from an angry wizard, or the curse that his death would leave in its wake," replied Ganieda.

"Don't think I didn't spot what you meant by an 'ancient heirloom' either!" I chided.

"And yet you haven't recognised where we are sitting?"

I looked up at the large rock, stood and studied it properly. There was a slender crack in the top of it. It was quite unremarkable really, unless you considered what might once have been stuck in it. I was briefly breathless, and sat back down heavily.

"It's all real?" I commented.

"Depends on what your version of reality is, Mr Pope. Maybe we only exist here because the stories were made in your realm? Or perhaps there are many worlds, and where they overlap remarkable things happen, and in turn get told as stories?

"I'm not certain it really matters."

I hadn't expected a philosophical portion to the quest, and it was unwelcome at that particular moment. I had enough to be thinking upon.

"Would you like to sleep before we continue? It might be best to take rest, as you have an ordeal before you," said Ganieda.

"You really think I'll be able to sleep after all this?"

"I can help with that." Ganieda reached over and gently touched my forehead. I don't recall deciding to try and sleep, I was simply unconscious. It was a dreamless slumber that seemed to last mere minutes, yet I woke refreshed and energised. It may have been the best sleep of my life. It was the last sleep of my old life.

We left the graveyard and entered another tunnel in the mist. I didn't understand how the daughter of the lake navigated them; there was nothing obvious marking them, and I got no feelings from them, magical or otherwise. My guess is that this realm had a different spectrum of vision, a variation in light that I was unable to detect.

We walked for much longer this time, and we did so in silence. There seemed very little for us to discuss. We both knew what must happen, and I wasn't concerned with the specifics of the task. Something nasty was to be aimed squarely at me and it was my job to accept that and bear the brunt as best I could. Some might try to claim heroism on my part, but I'll admit it was mostly curiosity. I had found myself within the pages of a legend; one does not turn away from a chance to become part of these stories. A life worth living lives on beyond its span. This was worth my life, if not for such selfish reasons as those, it was worth the attempt to save Britain, to clear it of sickness.

I had tried a few times to communicate with one of the mediums back at BOSS HQ, but wherever we were blocked the message. I'd never experienced this before, and I have had occasion to believe I have travelled beyond our mortal realm before. To my detriment, the fascination deepened as the danger mounted. Surely, that cannot be a healthy mindset!

Nevertheless, I was committed and I would see this through. A patch of light began to grow in front of us once again - it was our destination. No other stops had been mentioned. Ganieda had warned me that the journey would drain me, but I didn't feel bad at all. In fact, after my rest I felt better than I had for weeks. When we emerged from the tunnel I was surprised to find a scene lit by a thin sliver of moonlight. I tried to conjure a flame to light my way and failed. I looked at my hand, perplexed.

"I warned you that you would be drained by it," said Ganieda "Your powers will be diminished for some time. These are fairy roads, and bear a great cost. The lady has supplemented your power to allow you passage, but you will be quite defenceless for the next part of your task."

"Wonderful," I commented. I couldn't recall the last time I had been without magical power. I felt vulnerable and my fear grew. I realised with cold clarity that I had become dependent upon my powers, using them for quite simple tasks that might not truly require them. I wondered if I had made them a crutch. "Surely I will need power to open the cave, and break the seal?"

Ganieda smiled. "You know the heirloom that seals it. You are not as dull witted as you might pretend."

I wasn't pretending, so this stung me a little. She touched my head again, and at the lightest pressure I fell to one knee before her. Her hand dubbed my shoulders in turn and I felt a crackling sensation around my head. I looked up. Her hand signalled for me to rise.

"You are the only being now capable of removing the sword that seals the cave. Draw it from the rock like the great king of old once did and you will have completed the first part of your quest."

"Where must I go?" I asked.

She gestured to the right, and a thread of small lights suddenly flickered into being. "Follow the trail up the mountain to the cave." Ganieda paused. "I wish you luck Mr Pope. I am sorry this task fell to you, for I am not certain that you deserve this fate."

I smiled, trying my best to hide my nervousness. "My lady, do any of us truly get what we deserve? Some get more than their lot, most much less. Surely we can only be judged on what we make out of what comes our way?"

"Then I hope you make the very best out of what you are about to receive. My mother has foresight, she has waited many years to appoint this task, it is not an accident that you are here."

"Do you trust your mother's judgement, my lady?" I ventured.

Her laugh split the night air and threatened to bring the light of dawn. "Good sir, do you know any daughter that agrees completely with their mother? I may not trust her entirely, but I love her completely. I am sure she feels the same way about me. It is no fluke that I am your guide, for my mother knows my heart, my desires…"

With that she leaned forward, took me in a gentle but unyielding embrace and kissed me. I would not have pulled away even if the thought had crossed my mind. She was a most beautiful woman, and I dared not even think that she might look upon me in that way. The astonishment of the moment must have been wrought across my face as we parted. Again her laugh rang out into the darkness.

"Now go, Mr Pope. Consider that my blessing - I hope it will aid you in your task. I will return if you succeed." Ganieda drew her hood over her head and shielded her eyes from view. I wasn't sure, but I thought I spied a tear running down her cheek as she turned away from me.

I took a drink from my waterskin, careful to make sure it was the boiled water I had saved. It was disgusting compared to the draught the daughter of the lake had shared before. I looked around the landscape. It was nondescript in the darkness. I was high up on a hillside already. Rocky outcrops were visible; they looked like layers of stratified stone. The grass was long so I wasn't following a well-worn path. The string of lights reminded me of the ones that had faded in and out within the misty tunnels. As I passed them they flared blue and disappeared. The landscape below was flat and featureless in the gloom. Mists swirled and rose, seeming to touch everywhere in this place. I studied the moon and stars carefully. I wasn't certain but I believed that I had come back into the mortal realm again, and that this place existed within our world.

The night confused me as I had no way of knowing what day it was, and how long I had been in the other place with the Lady of the Lake and her kin. I wondered if the churchyard where we rested had also been in the 'real' world. Maybe it was a construct to underpin the lake daughter's story?

I think back upon this adventure many times and know unswervingly how simple it was for the tales of legend to be remembered and recounted, yet they seem so at odds and contradictory. There is a confusion of realms overlapping, no stable timeline, and no way to fully comprehend the powers at play. You get to recall your fragment of the story, while feeling it is only a small part of a much greater and complex whole.

The ramble up the hillside was quite refreshing. I could actually see progress as a result of my steps, instead of feeling as though I was walking upon the same spot as I had been in the mist tunnels. The wind was keen, but not chill. If I hadn't felt as though I was walking towards my doom it would have been rather pleasant.

The string of lights stopped at a rock face. We were close to the top of the hill; it looked as though the slope wound around it a few more turns. The cliff I was standing by rose for a good twenty feet.

I was expecting to see something obvious here. The instructions had been simple. But I suppose there had to be some form of camouflage about the cave entrance and the seal, or it would be too easily discovered. I fished in my pocket for a seeing stone. I may not have had any power, but I still had a few objects that held their own.

I lifted the smooth stone with a hole at its centre to my eye. Immediately I saw the trail of lights that I had followed here ignited once more, and there in the centre of the wall at chest height, an old weathered sword hilt protruding from the rock.

Reaching out with my free hand I grasped the handle. It was warm, which disquieted me. I felt crackling around my head again, fizzes and pops near my ears. When I looked up there was a strobing of lights. I wondered if there appeared to be something above me that moved with my head? Power surged through my body to my hand; I felt my grip fuse to the hilt, and without any effort on my part I began to draw the blade from the stone. There was no noise, no friction.

I stood before the rock face and held the large sword in front of me. As I looked down the blade its appearance changed, the years of exposure melting from it. Excalibur appeared before me as though it was newly forged. The blade itself began to shine, the intensity of the light almost blinding. I wished to close my eyes but could not. Within the light words appeared in a script I didn't recognise but could read clearly. They spelled out 'Take me up'. I turned the blade over to see the other side (again with no thought or action on my part) where it was written: 'Cast me away'.

The light dimmed, and I was once again upon a hillside in the darkness, though I could see the magic at play all around me without the help of my stone.

The crack in which the sword had laid began to extend and widen. There was a gentle crumbling and rumbling from deep within the cliff-face. I expected there to be a heavy grinding or sliding of some ancient mechanism, but the crack simply parted the rock, making an entrance big enough that I might walk though it with a stoop.

I felt absurd holding the great sword of legend, but realised it was the only weapon I had for whatever might await me inside the cave. I took it in both hands and raised it to a simple guard before entering the blackness of the stony prison.

The sword gave off an eerie glow that lit my way. The entry walls were as smooth as glass but still showed the layered pattern of the rock. A few feet in, the walls began to roughen and take on a more natural appearance. As soon as I was past that initial entrance I was hit with a blast of energy.

It struck me in the chest and threw me back out of the cave. The site of the impact stung and lingered; from there I felt a wave of sensation flowing away to cover my entire body. I was shaking and convulsing. Then I felt a numbness on my lips. It was cold, and that feeling emanated from my head all over me to stop my jerking limbs.

I was finally still. I took huge wracking breaths into my lungs; through the whole ordeal I hadn't been able to breathe, cry out, or even see properly.

I had no idea what had hit me.

I tried moving and found, to my surprise, that I could. There was still an ache in my chest, but there was no physical sign of injury or distress. I had not let go of the sword, and was still gripping it firmly.

I wondered if I had to go back in. I'd opened the cave, I had the sword. Surely I could leave and my obligations were fulfilled? I didn't know if I had been struck by the wizard himself, or by some trap left by the Lady of the Lake for anyone that managed to open her prison.

I recalled the old quest stories. There were always times when the knights could have turned back, returned without a stain upon their honour, but they carried on, knowing it was the right thing to do.

I hoisted the weapon once more, and entered the cave. This time I felt a change in the atmosphere as I crossed the threshold. There had been a field of some kind within the cave; I had been struck when I broke it.

I lifted the sword higher, trying to light the cave interior. It was much smaller than I imagined it might be from the outside; barely ten paces across, and fifteen deep. There were scratches on the wall - strange pictograms, and writing. I didn't recognise the forms. At the far end there was a makeshift cot and a small pile of books. It seemed Nimue had taken pity on her teacher at some point and allowed him something to read.

As for signs of the wizard himself I couldn't see any, until I studied the floor closer. There was a discolouration to the ground in one particular patch. Dust. Possibly ashes? I assumed the remains of a single body lost to the ages.

Merlin was indeed dead.

I heard a noise near the cave entrance. I turned, leading with the sword, to find Ganieda standing there. Her eyes wide with surprise.

I lowered the weapon. "Apologies, my lady. I was startled."

She composed herself quickly. "Not at all, Mr Pope. I'm glad to see you have succeeded in your task." She cast her gaze around the cave, lingering on the patch of discoloured soil near the centre. "Mother will be pleased," she said. I was not convinced by her tone. Something seemed wrong in the moment, but I did not dare ask.

"I was struck by something when I entered. I cannot explain what happened," I said.

"It was the curse my mother warned you of, Mr Pope. We should return to her. She will want to see you." With that she turned from the cave.

I followed, part of me wishing I could stay to study what was on the walls. I felt there was either great wisdom there to be revealed, or it was the ravings of a sexually frustrated man driven to solitary madness. I willed myself to remember the forms, the writings. To this day I cannot bring any of it to mind. It is as if those specific memories have been expunged from my mind, or worse - are there, but hidden.

I exited the cave and the fresh air hit my face like a slap. I had not realised how close it was inside. There was a pressure within, a brooding atmosphere that was uncomfortable. Ganieda was standing in the mouth of a fairy road, waiting. Apparently, there was no need to descend the hill.

I tucked the most famous sword in history and legend into my belt like a child's toy, and followed. I have never felt quite so absurd.

I don't know what the difference was on the return trip, but I could feel the nature of the tunnel grating against me. Draining the power from me as I walked. I don't know where the power inside me was coming from, I still felt empty, but something was being taken to pay for my passage - and it was being taken in huge lumps. This journey was far more direct and costly.

I wondered what the rush was for?

We emerged into the milky light of the bridge across the western end of the lake around Glastonbury Tor.

Ganieda turned to me. "Time to fulfil your oath."

It took me a moment to realise what she meant. "Really? You want me to…"

She nodded, and smiled sheepishly, though a note of concern never left her eyes.

I drew Excalibur from my belt, and held it up one last time to inspect it - feel the light it emitted caress my face, the power of it in my grasp.

I drew my arm back and flung the sword off the bridge and out over the calm lake.

As the sword spiralled down from the apex of my throw the waters began to move and, inevitably, a hand rose to catch Excalibur by the hilt. For a moment it was held aloft above the lapping current. It shone, its beauty radiant against the ripples of the lake, then slowly it descended to be swallowed completely by the water.

Almost instantly, a vortex appeared below us and Nimue rose to speak with us. Excalibur was nowhere to be seen.

"Mr Pope, you have fulfilled your quest. I am glad. It has been long ages since I was last the least bit surprised." Nimue looked amused for a split second before fury clouded her features. "You should be dead."

"I have no doubt of that, my lady," I replied. "As you warned, I was struck by a curse upon entering the cave, but some force quelled its effect upon me. I cannot explain it. I do not usually like to use the term, but I cannot believe it is anything but good fortune."

"No, Mr Pope. You were saved by weakness." The Lady of the Lake cast her gaze towards her daughter. Ganieda stood, her head bowed with her hood raised, a stance and demeanour of contrition. "Weakness and pity. Isn't this true, my daughter?"

A small voice replied. "Yes, Mother. I have failed you."

"This was your test too. If the mortal succeeded, I needed a method to help him; for him to succeed unscathed you would have had to offer him your assistance. You have sealed your own fate," said Nimue. She was not particularly angry, but a sadness radiated from her.

I was dumbfounded, my wits slow to fit the pieces of the lady's plan together. "You came to the cave to recover the sword, expecting me to have died, didn't you?" I asked Ganieda.

The only response I received was a slight nod.

"Yes. The curse should have claimed your life, Mr Pope," said Nimue. "I believe it would have without interference. I have long suspected that Merlin took the choice to die, but his power is not something that easily fades from the world. That power should have consumed you, and escaped the prison.

"But with my daughter's blessing it seems you have survived. Do you feel it within you still?"

I considered the question. As I had passed through the fairy path, it had felt different. I kindled a flame in my palm to test my powers. It felt effortless, as though I had to simply think about what to do instead of cast spells and forms. "I do," I answered.

Nimue chuckled. "Before you get carried away thinking you have the full power of Merlin I will disabuse you of the notion. Most of that power escaped through you, like a lightning rod. It has gone back to the land, but it has left you a gift… or indeed a curse, as I promised you."

"It will be a curse for him," said Ganieda.

"Yes, I suppose it will. And you, my daughter, will get to watch it torture him, and never be able to provide aid again. That will be your punishment for disobedience, for I will fulfil my promise. You will go with Mr Pope to heal the damage that was done to the waters of Britain. Then you will take your place as the new spirit of the Thames, forgoing your physical shell and giving yourself to the land as a pure elemental spirit."

"Yes, Mother," replied Ganieda through tears.

"I will thank you for your service, Mr Pope, and I will even apologise for the conduct of my daughter. I fear that you will look back upon this moment many years from now, and feel that she has done you a great disservice. I believe we will meet again.

"To you, my daughter I say farewell, for you will never be able to return to me here, though I will feel your energy flow to me until the end of all things. Be comforted by one thing; this fate was borne of your own choices."

With that the Lady of the Lake descended to her watery realm, and then a tentacle of liquid rose and deposited a small satchel next to Ganieda. She promptly picked it up, slung it across her shoulder, and walked into the mists.

I followed, quite helplessly, not knowing what I should have taken from the conversation. Though, as it turned out, I had plenty of time to find out.

We came back to Glastonbury Tor as I had seen it before. The mists had thinned and the ground was visible. I had no idea of the date or time. It seemed to be late morning by the position of the sun.

Ganieda looked wistfully across the plain to the imposing hill. I'm not sure she saw the same view I did. "I will never see the waters of my home again," she said under her breath.

"I'm sorry to have caused you such difficulty, my lady Ganieda," I offered.

She turned to me, a brave smile upon her lips and tears upon her cheeks. "No, Mr Pope, it is I that owe you the apology. You do not know the full horror of your predicament, and I will not tell you until it is time for us to part. That will be my self-imposed punishment, as it will be harder to do so by then. For now we will journey together to set right what has been done."

And that is what we did. There were no fairy roads, barely any magic at all, in truth. We travelled simply, as quickly as we might. I felt an urgency to begin the cleanse, but there was a reticence in my companion, as though she wished to draw the process out - as though she was delaying the inevitable completion of the task.

We started in Sunderland, where it had all begun. I led her to the stretch of river where Jenkins had lost his fingers to the Groac'h. Ganieda seemed to sense where the Naiad egg was located without my direction.

I had no idea how long the spirit inside needed to gestate, but I was sure I could see movement within the glowing, golden shell.

The daughter of the lake never touched the intruding egg. She fished a hand into the bag her mother had given her and dropped a freshwater pearl into the current. It sank to the riverbed and settled; it carried far more weight than it looked. I wondered if my companion's burden was much greater than I supposed.

A thumping gust of energy thrust from the pearl and it dissolved into the water, the stream carrying it away. The initial energy burst struck the Naiad egg and it too dissolved.

In the distance something surfaced. I heard the ringing laughter of a child, and playful splashing. It waved a hand in our direction, which was returned by Ganieda with a proud smile. The young Naiad dived back under and was gone. I'd like to say it was as if she was never there, but that wasn't true. Something had certainly changed.

In my heart I knew that the river was being cleansed.

We repeated this process in every river that had been tainted by the Rhinedaughter. It took us months, and over that time I became close with the daughter of the lake. I will not delve into the details of those memories, for I wish to keep hold of my feelings. They are precious to me. I will not filter them through the Sentiment Stone.

I could write about it without the stone, of course, but some things do not need to be shared.

The one part of my time with Ganieda I will gladly commit to this pulp through the stone is our parting. For the bitterness of it lingers within my heart, and I do not think the stain of it will ever be removed for as long as I live.

We had travelled the nation together, rebalancing nature, clearing the disease that had been dubbed 'cholera' from the waters. There was only the Thames left, and we both knew that there were no more pearls in the bag that was given by Nimue.

The final offering would be Ganieda herself. Her weakness, as perceived by her mother, was interest and pity towards mortals. She saw the tragedy of our relatively short lives, and wondered at how hard we strived to make something out of the time we were each given. It fascinated her.

She explained that it was not only pity that had prompted her to save me that fateful day, but the beginnings of love, for she sensed the chivalric ethos of the knights of old reborn in me. I record that statement as one of the kindest compliments I have ever had the pleasure to receive.

We chose to part on London Bridge.

Our journey had taken longer than it should have. We were selfish, taking as much time to be together as we possibly could. I bear the cost of this selfish choice when I think of the countless people that might have died due to our delay. But I would not change it. May the devil take me. I would not.

Ganieda took my hands in hers. "The time has come, and my mother's words prove themselves to be true. This is the bitterest punishment. I will be with you always, as part of the city you call home, but we will never be together again as we have been on our journey."

She stifled a sob. Tears also pricked my own eyes. I couldn't look away from her, even though I knew it was causing her discomfort; she did not want me to see her in pain. I would have done anything to take it from her.

"For as long as I live I will treasure this time we have had. I will remember it always," I said.

She bowed her head, unable to look at me. "You may not be able to keep that promise, Silas. The last task I have in this part of my life is to reveal to you the nature of your curse.

"It is immortality.

"You will endure far beyond your natural lifespan. You may still be harmed, still be slain by injury or wound. But time will not lay its marks upon you. I am sorry, for my actions have served you this fate."

I had felt the increased power over time, and I had noticed the aches and pains in my legs and back had lessened to almost nothing, but we had been walking rather a lot. I simply thought I was getting into decent shape. Initially I really couldn't see why she was calling it a curse!

"Surely it is a blessing?" I said.

She looked up at me with the most profound sadness in her eyes. It broke a part of me that has never mended. "Mortals are special because their lives end. Dying is a gift. Lingering beyond your years will be a curse. You will watch friends and loved ones die, you will see your world change beyond recognition, and you will never feel as though you belong. And I know you, Silas. I know your heart. You will not release yourself from service; you will not choose to die while you believe you can still make a difference. For you this is locking you into an eternity of servitude, an eternity of loneliness.

"I should have let you die, it would have been a kindness."

We hugged one last time, and we kissed tenderly. There seemed to be no more words to say.

The daughter of the lake dived from the bridge. A tremor rippled across the water as she broke the surface, and I never saw her again.

Of course the river was cleansed, and it was once again protected. I often went down to the banks, dipped my feet into the lapping current, and tried to commune with the spirit that I once knew. She had changed, but I recognised a part of her.

Over time I sensed that my visits pained her and I stopped. Her mother's punishment was harsh and unfair.

I intend to keep my promise though. I will remember my time with Ganieda for as long as I live, and it turns out that may be a very long time, indeed.

ꠧꠛ꠷ꠛꠗꠗꠗꠗ ꠛꠛ

The effect of the stone is amazing.

Those simple lines that produced such intense feelings are now softened. I can think about what happened without breaking. There is still pain, but I'm not driven mad by it.

Mr Hopkins tells me that if I write a fuller account I can be free of my emotions while keeping my memories. This seems like an ideal solution. The stone is warm in my hand. I have gripped it so hard that it has left impressions in my palm.

I'm not religious, but I am ready to confess.

Mother became ill quite suddenly.

She was feverish and short of breath. Father sent for a doctor. I asked the Order if they had any connections that might bring better treatment. We spent every penny we had to try medicines and treatments, all to no avail.

She suffered, it seemed, with no end. I won't lie - I wished for death to take her, for her suffering to end. I know my father contemplated taking action. He would brood and pace before flying into a rage and leaving the house.

We didn't have the strength.

I did try to find an alternative solution. Every spare moment was spent in the Order library seeking help. I read about a huge variety of medicinal approaches, from healing herb poultices and inhalants to practical rituals.

I started small. The Order may have guessed my intentions to become a practitioner. They didn't stop me. Part of me wishes they had. I often wonder if they were secretly pleased. Nobody else had dared to make any attempts to use the knowledge we debated and shared. Out of natural learned curiosity, I'm certain they took interest in my experiments. In hindsight, I think it likely that Mr Hopkins may have had a hand in it too.

Nothing was working. All of the natural remedies and mixes gave only temporary relief. It was something. We would get a part of Mother back in short bursts. My father was overjoyed to find hope. He pushed and encouraged me to continue. I didn't need much, in truth. My ambitions were escalating all the time. The more I read, the more I understood (or thought I did) the more I began to believe I could find a way to save her.

It was my hubris that killed them.

The day I decided to cross a threshold over which I will never be able to return was notable. It was the same day the French Queen lost her head. I saw the headlines on the papers as I smuggled a book out of the Order's library. I needed it in front of me to make my attempt.

I had been researching a branch of power called 'borrowing'. It only came to mind as something I had skimmed over in my reading after overhearing a passing comment from my father to my mother. She was insensible - in a fever. "I wish I could take the pain away. I would endure it myself rather than watch you suffer," my father whispered to her through tears.

I continued my research, and once I believed that my plan might be possible I sat my father down to ask him if he had meant what he said.

"We can share Mother's illness between us. Life is energy; it flows between living things at all times. There are ways to dissolve some of the barriers between us and release the energies that usually cannot travel. This can include maladies." I looked my father square in the eye. The look of hope etched into his features broke my heart. "We can share her burden. Spread across all three of us, we have a better chance of fighting the illness. We could all recover, or it could take us all. But Mother would have a fighting chance."

This was the moment, as a thirteen year old boy, I became the adult in my family. Perhaps it had quietly happened over time, as my knowledge grew and my parents let me go into a world they couldn't understand. It was the moment my father should have been the responsible one; told me no.

He trusted my intellect. He trusted my capabilities. He was wrong.

It makes me sick to think of it now. The idea of anything going wrong never occurred to him. It was a solution, a possibility. Desperation is a terrible aid to judgement.

The principle I was exploring, theoretically, was quite simple. There are many different realms that exist all in one place at the same time. We cannot see or touch them, but they are there. It is possible to link to those realms and exchange energies. Something happens in this exchange. The energies work more efficiently in a realm that they are not native to. If I give a bit this side, I get much more back from the other, and vice-versa. This amplification of energy would enable me to perform the rite that would share my mother's burden between us.

I say 'us' - in a moment of parental clarity, my father insisted that only he should take the illness. His reasoning was sound; I needed to concentrate on the magic. It also gave us a fallback plan. If it was not enough, if my mother didn't improve or my father was overcome, there was still the option that I could take their pain through a repeat of the ritual. The first attempt would be a test.

A failed test.

We arranged my parent's room. Emptied it, aside from the bed that was dragged off centre. My mother was insensible. A small blessing. I don't believe she ever knew what happened. I hope she doesn't know what I did.

I drew circles on the floor; a large one around the bed, and two smaller ones in which my father and I would stand. These were connected. Then began the painstaking task of rendering the correct runes and symbols around and across the simple framework. It took me two days to complete, with very little rest. I should have rested.

The text from which I was taking instructions described the necessary state of being that had to be achieved by the magician to initiate the ritual. It was something I had been practising for some time beforehand as it came up a lot in my reading. The description varied, but a similar theme of traits was always present. It described the atmosphere I first experienced when I watched Mr Walton's spirit leave his body; a thickening of the atmosphere, a stillness upon nature.

I had been meditating, trying to achieve this state. I managed to do it for split seconds at a time. I thought it would be enough to open the way.

My hand is cramping. Sweat is pouring off my brow as I write. The ink is blotted with drops falling from my nose. Tears no longer mar my words. This experience can live inside me no longer.

I will not stop now.

I sat my father in his circle and handed him a knife.

I approached my mother, made a cut across her palm, and let it hang from the bed. Blood dripped onto the floor and the markings I had made. She barely reacted.

I stood in my own circle.

"Do not leave the ring, Father. It is vital," I warned. Not for the first time. I had drummed it into him. I had tried to explain what he might see, what he might feel. He was as ill prepared for what happened as I was.

On a count we cut our own hands to let drops fall on the connecting lines that ran between us all.

I tried to slip into the trance. The pain in my hand was a distraction, the pressure of the moment relentless. I felt my father's sad hopeful eyes upon me.

Then all was still and silent.

I opened my eyes. The air was thick, the colours of the room muted, except for the blood that was on the floor and running from our hands. That glowed with a hungry intensity.

I took the bloody knife, held it in front of me and made a small cut in the air. It was like slicing through jelly. The wound in the air shone with a bright yellow light. As I pushed deeper, the colour changed to green.

I had read about this. Each realm shone with a different light. I wasn't certain which one I needed. I had picked up on the idea that the deeper I delved, the more power I could mine.

I put more pressure on the blade. The light flickered in different shades, until it stopped in an eerie red. The knife was almost lost in the air to its handle. I twisted it to open the cut and establish the portal.

The blood was sucked from the knife into the other world. I held my hand out to it, feeding it.

The air around the opening loosened a little, and began to melt to liquid. A puddle was hanging in front of me with a red wound at its centre. The knife handle lingered in space, though that felt like the least of the oddities.

I looked to my parents. They seemed to me as though they were frozen inside the solid atmosphere. If I concentrated I could see my father moving very slowly. I wondered if the magic was having a strange effect on how I experienced time.

The hole sucked the blood from the floor in a fragile line. The liquid thread connected the markings on the floor to the unknown realm. The red light flowed along it and travelled along the markings. The air around the symbols and lines melted, bringing everything within the defined pattern into the same state of being as me.

My father became animated. His face wore a look of wonder.

We were linked by the power of the other realm. The energy flowed between us. I felt linked to my parents in a way I couldn't properly explain. I felt their breath in my lungs, our hearts beat in the same rhythm.

Now came the most delicate part of the process. I had to define the malignant energy within my mother, split it, and push some of it across the link to my father.

The power flowing into me was immense and intoxicating. Any weariness burned away. It was the most alive I had ever felt. I was connected to the universe in a new way - like looking up at the stars in the sky and realising how small you are.

It all felt so natural. I knew what to do. I shaped my fingers to control the flow of energy, pick through my mother's body, seeking out the illness, the pain. I held it all in my hand. The temptation to simply rip it all from her tickled my thoughts.

The only thing stopping me was the knowledge that energy cannot be taken without it being replaced. There is a balance.

I took pieces and pushed them towards my father. As they flowed into him, parts of his own energy trickled back to Mother.

It was working.

Excitement surged through me. I was going to save my mother. I could see it all so clearly, the energies flowing between us. I understood our nature; what makes us human. I was playing with our very souls.

I wondered briefly if I had the right.

The knife, hanging in mid air, fell to the ground as the gap it had wedged open widened suddenly. A clawed hand gripped the edges of the portal, scrabbling for purchase.

Horror sank to the pit of my stomach.

The hand grasped the tendril of my blood that linked the gateway to my incantation. I felt a new energy entering the ritual. It was dark, heavy. It felt like the illness, but magnified many times over. The hand faded as the energy completed its transference. It was heading for my mother.

I panicked and quickly shifted all of my mother's energy down the line into my father. I needed to protect her.

I couldn't manipulate the new energy that had entered the spell. It had an agency of its own. It paused by my mother's hand before climbing that thread and entering her body.

My mother's body moved more than it had in a month. But it was unnatural; it moved in a jerky uncomfortable way, as though it couldn't do what it was being instructed to. Her eyes opened and they were pure black. I felt the trickle of urine run down my leg. My father was shouting, but I couldn't hear the words.

Bile burned my throat as I witnessed a creature shed my mother's body like a costume of flesh. It struck her likeness away with clawed hands to reveal its true image. A skeletal form with thin, greasy skin stretched taut over its frame. The hands were the same as the one that had probed the portal. Its head was shrunken, with large dark eyes and no mouth.

My father screamed and stepped out of his circle. The spell around him and the line that had linked my mother disappeared. It was broken.

Somewhere in him was my mother's soul, and her illness, but in this moment my father was consumed with rage and grief. He ran to the ring that circled Mother's bed.

I screamed at him, I pleaded. I can't remember the words I used, I can't recall hearing my own voice. As soon as Father left the circle, the air around him thickened again, and he was obscured.

I watched it all happen. It was so very strange and terrible.

The creature was still in my time. I saw it approach the circle. It probed it with a claw, then a hand. It threw itself against it. It couldn't pass through. I felt a small tingle of relief. I needed to do something. I realised I'd been a witness to all of this instead of actively trying to stop it, even though I had no idea how.

If one creature could find the link to the realm, surely there could be more? I decided to close the portal and hope I had enough power to right my wrongs. I severed the tendril of blood from the opening and swirled my finger in the watery air. I created a whirlpool that slowly closed the hole at the centre.

The creature sensed what I was doing and became panicked and furious. It beat its body against the invisible wall between us.

From my perspective, I saw my father, inch by inch, crossing the room towards the creature's circle. He couldn't hear me now. I couldn't stop him. The creature noticed too.

As the hole sealed, my father reached the perimeter of the large circle. Thankfully, he didn't seem able to enter it from the outside just as the creature couldn't exit it from within.

The distorted shape of my father was against the invisible barrier. I could only assume he was beating his fists against it, trying in vain to get to the creature, or save mother. I couldn't imagine what he saw inside the circle. If his movements were slow to me, perhaps our movements inside the circles were faster, maybe even a blur of activity? He certainly didn't seem to see the danger he was in as the creature crossed the ring and stood in front of him. The barrier had no thickness - they were virtually touching.

The creature pressed its hand against the barrier where my father was touching it. Slowly the hand moved. Inch by inch it travelled through the barrier, into my father's body.

All I saw after that was the creature leaping around and around, up and down within the enclosure, its arm through the barrier, as though it was tethered to a weight on the other side. My father seemed to stay in the same place that the creature had grabbed him.

I felt the energies shift. The creature had drained everything from my father. Everything.

Tears streamed down my face. My emotions made my concentration falter, but not long enough for the power to dissipate.

The creature's arm was still stuck in the barrier. It wrenched and writhed against it. I watched as it pulled itself apart, ripping skin and bone with its claws, leaving its limb hanging in mid-air. A thick, dark fluid seeped from its wound. It crawled over to the line in the markings that joined our circles, and let the fluid gush onto it.

The malevolent energy began to transfer back into the spell. The creature was coming for me. Its broken and weak body lay in the circle, its energy massing in the link. I felt it creeping back across towards me.

I willed it to stop, to block it somehow. I bent all my thought on it. The dark energy flowed slowly towards me and stopped a few inches from my circle.

Sweat stood out on my forehead from effort. My eyes were riveted on the glowing line. Time lost all meaning.

In my peripheral vision I noticed changes in the slow-motion world beyond the solid air. My father's body moved slowly around the creature's circle. Up, down, round and around, tracing the movements the creature had made before it had clawed its arm free. Each movement of my father's body left a red stain behind it.

I realised what was happening. I was witnessing my father's death played out to me in excruciating detail.

I don't know how long it lasted. How long I was stuck like that; stuck between fending off the creature, and watching my father's body being broken and spread around the room. I tried to detach my mind. I pretended I was dead. I considered giving in to the dark energy and letting it take me. Joining my parents. Accepting the punishment for my actions.

I was insensible when the end came. So much so that I didn't recognise it as an end. I have been stuck in a semi-conscious nightmare state for weeks, possibly months. I don't know how long it has been.

I have only recently begun to have moments of lucidity. Moments that Mr Hopkins has used to try and explain what happened.

Sometimes I believe I am dead. That the creature took me, and this is my purgatory, maybe my Hell.

Of course it was Mr Hopkins that saved me, or at least rescued me. I was correct in my assumption that The Order of the Inner Dawn had been on instructions to let me experiment. Somebody was interested in finding out what I might be capable of.

Mr Furlong was an informant. There is a secret organisation that monitors the use of magic and protects the Empire from its effects. Mr Hopkins belongs to it. He was interested in me as a possible recruit. Apparently he still is.

When Mr Hopkins was informed of my research and what I thought were secret actions, he made sure that I was monitored by a spiritual medium. As soon as I opened the portal to the other realm, he was told and hurried to my home.

The differences in time are difficult to grasp. My mind holds them, but the facts are slippery. Mr Hopkins got to that room within twenty minutes. I felt as though I fought off the creature's dark energy for days. I watched my father get ripped apart for a week... drifted through that waking nightmare for months.

Mr Hopkins entered the room. It was covered in blood and viscera. There were only two clean circles on the floor. One containing me, the other held my mother's broken body and the remains of the creature. He explained how he broke my spell and exorcised the demon, as though it was simplicity itself.

I didn't feel any relief, I didn't know it was over. I was just an orphan laying on the floor in my own waste, babbling to myself. I was broken.

I'm not sure I'll ever be fixed.

Acknowledgements

𝕾𝖅𝕬𝕶𝕯𝕲𝕷𝕾𝕿𝖃𝕾𝕮𝕾𝕶𝖁𝕾

This book wouldn't have been made without the support of everyone that showed interest in it over on my Patreon page. I wrote a short story to post each month as an extension of my comic book, Cognition.

A small inbuilt audience that showed up every month to read what I was putting together gave me huge motivation. Thank you to: Nic Sage, GMark Cole, Michael Rider, Dan Baptista, Kevin Povey, Xavier Hugonet, Matt Harsha, Shaun Hastings and Sean Carson Hull.

A special mention should go to my constant sounding boards, Chris Sides, Steve Horry and Jimmy Furlong, they are generous with their encouragement but also inspirational when they share their own projects with me.

David Hailwood took this manuscript and knocked it into grammatical shape, his editorial eye is something I constantly aspire to. John Ottaway proof-read, giving invaluable insight and feedback.

Everyone the project touched on its way to this final format has helped shape it. Any mistakes in these pages are wholly my own.

Of course, I must thank Claire and Delilah, because without them there really isn't much point in anything else.

Ken Reynolds
Ipswich, UK - June 2020

Also available:

"With terrific, fully fleshed characters driving some truly atmospheric stories and gorgeous gothic art, Cognition feels unique compared to anything currently in comics."

James Blundell, Pipedream Comics

www.kenreynolds.co.uk

www.kenreynolds.bigcartel.com

 @ReynoldsKR20

Printed in Great Britain
by Amazon